My Husband Wants to Keep Me Dominant

Sam Wicker

Books by Sam Wicker

I'm No Hero Trilogy
I'm No Hero
I'm Your Hero
I'm His Hero (2026)

The My Husband Wants Series
My Husband Wants to Keep Me Pristine
My Husband Wants to Keep Me Dominant
My Husband Wants to Keep Me Gay (soon)
My Husband Wants to Keep Me Sated (soon)

Standalones
The Bell Earth Witch

My Husband
Wants to Keep Me
Dominant

Dedication

To those who prefer to laugh instead of cry, and those who need
an escape.

Xensis
Serland
Norvasos
King's Island
Capital
Telkenlan
Deadlands
Gavaintch
Ichie
Immortal Lands
Gachent
Queen's Rest

Content Warning

This book includes content that may be triggering for some readers. Read at your discretion. Content warnings: gore, war, allusions to incest, allusions to rape, familial homicide, allusions to teen sex, traumatic child birth, death of a mother to a newborn, BDSM, and genetic disease.

Chapter 1: Whips and Cups

"Harder!" The slap of the leather upon flesh broke the rhythm of grunts, pants, and soft feminine cries. The thongs slid over the sweaty tanned back with pink welts as the muscles gathered and released to pick up the order with gusto.

"Yes, Mistress," the redhead turned his head. His heated gaze pierced through the low candlelit room, resting on her as his body undulated fully to make his hips thrust his cock harder and deeper into the woman under him.

His audacity made her want him, but she must keep to her role.

And her chastity.

Striding forward, the heels of her riding boots clacking against the cracked wooden floorboards, she put the butt of the whip under his chin, turning his head up so he met her gaze. She placed a boot on his ass after hiking her white skirts up to her knees to reveal the thick, tooled leather and a slash of pale thigh.

His thrusts stilled, pressed fully into the woman beneath him, who whimpered and mewled as she rocked her hips to keep her own pleasure alive.

She leaned down, putting her face in his, the nose of the mask poking his right cheek. "I told you to focus on your whore, sir."

"She's had an orgasm. Don't you want one, Mistress Garnet?" He asked, a glint in his dark eyes.

Her thoughts drifted to how his hand warmed the small of her back earlier when he'd ushered her into the room. The length of his cock before he'd sheathed it in Clover, how did it feel? "You haven't the money to take my first, sir. Nor do I think you're worthy since you cannot manage the simplest of orders. Tell me, is he good enough for you?"

"Yes," Clover said with a moan, still undulating under the lord. The sling's slow movements slid him in and out of her.

She watched the muscles in his arms move with each swing and knew he was helping Clover remain fucked despite his mistress halting them. Insubordinate. She gripped his long tresses and hauled back while keeping her foot on the left globe of his taut ass.

His hands flew to his hair as his back arched.

The lord's hiss of pain made her lick her lips. He had the best sounds of all her clients. The best body, too.

"Mistress, I should warn you, there are tips..."

A few bit into her palm, but she didn't mind. The mistress jerked him further back, bending him over the length of her leg so the back of his head rested on the top of her knee-high boot. "I didn't permit you to speak so freely."

Clover took full advantage, gripping those narrow hips between her legs and riding her way to climax.

"No, Mistress. You did not." The redhead stated between pants.

His partner cried out her release and lay in the swing with a smile as she reveled in the orgasm.

"Finish yourself." She said, hovering over him before her balance tilted from the odd position. Her boot heel clacked back on the floor, and she grew steadier on both feet. He hadn't moved to obey. Instead, his eyes were up, watching her, hands still in his hair, fingers touching hers.

With a flick of her wrist, the leather thongs smacked his flat stomach, taut with the strain of bending backwards. His body jerked, but he didn't make another move to comply. His tongue trailed over his lips, gaze still on her.

"May I speak, Mistress?"

She raised a brow; the sweat damp mask pulling tight. "Should I allow him, Clover?"

"He might've a good idea, hm?" Clover's twang snaked out as she watched a spot on the ceiling, swinging gently in the straps of cloth hung from the rafters.

"Speak." She demanded, and returned to stare into his dark eyes. A glimmer appeared there, as if they held their own internal fire within the depths.

Sam Wicker

"Let my mouth give you an orgasm. It'd be better than your fingers after I leave." Another smirk twisted his lips. "Trust me."

"Since he's worthy of you, Clover, do you think I should sate his thirst?" She had to play the part. Keep to her act. No matter how the redhead looked or what he did to her nethers, she was his dom.

The bastard knew she was wet. Who wouldn't be? All the whores fought for him. The rare redhead, the rarer long tresses, and a body that promised all sorts of power. She was one of three Mistresses he hadn't broken.

"Oh, aye."

Clover was of no aid.

She felt her eyes narrow as he grinned. Already thinking he'd won. She smiled and loosened her hold on his hair. Using the whip's handle, she beckoned him as she stepped away.

He shifted, every muscle in his body taut as he turned from bending over backwards, to walking on his hands and knees before her.

The tiny space contained the swing, tiny desk, a wobbly chair, plus a narrow couch lacking a back. In two steps, she bumped into the softest piece of furniture. "Stay."

She waited until he stilled, sitting back on his heels, before disengaging her hand from his tresses. Slowly she gathered her dress, all lace and cotton, and pulled them up to free her legs up to her knees. She threw her leg over the couch, straddling it, before sitting and leaning back against the threadbare arm. Her skirts were dangerously high, sending a thrill through her while embarrassment threatened to ruin the moment.

She dropped the bunched cloth, flicking the whip languidly at her side as her other hand trailed up her bare thigh, until the damp heat of herself pressed against the back of her thumb. "You've gone soft. Fix it."

He was ready to obey this time. His palm slaking down his Clover-orgasm slick cock. With a few pumps, and his dark eyes steady on her hand between her legs, his manhood revived, standing tall.

"Remove your hand. Let me see."

Again, such quick compliance.

"Tell me, whipping boy, do you thirst?" She snapped the whip against the back of the couch, letting her arm rest above her head as she slid down the length of the worn furniture. Every inch bared more thigh, but she stopped before her core could be viewed.

"I do, Mistress."

She liked that tone. The one where he was on the verge of breaking the little thread of control. A tiny shard of fear pricked through the adrenaline of having a man on his knees before her. What if she pushed him too hard, and he lost control? Could she keep him off long enough for Clover to regain dominance or for her to grab Nathan or Sawyer?

Would she still be intact by the waking morn? She should end this farce. But she didn't want to. Was it such a catastrophe if a man discovered their new wife possessed prior experience?

"Mistress Garnet?"

Of all the fuck gods, she'd gotten lost in thought. "Do you want to drink?" She flicked her fingers; her skirts still gripped in them, just shy of giving him a glance of the cup.

"Desperately."

Oh, that was bad. That look. The desperation in his voice.

She switched her gaze from him to Clover, better to clear her mind. The other woman nodded and got up. Her partner opened the door and motioned.

Two bulky forms filled the doorway, then the room, following Clover in like shadows. Nathan was the broadest and tallest of the two, his bald head shining black in the candlelight, his shirt a stark contrast of white against ebony. Sawyer wasn't much smaller, and the metal-plated gloves he wore took away any hopes patrons had of taking out the pale man.

The Mistress raised her palm, halting them as the naked female walked toward her. She smiled up at Clover and asked, "Remember that one time you helped Opal?"

Clover grinned and settled herself behind, but a little to the side of Garnet.

"Stay there. Or they will end the show for you." She said, before returning her gaze to the lord still on his knees before her.

"Wha..." he began, then stilled when Clover's fingers slid into where his eyes rested.

She arched and moaned as fingers found her clit and rubbed in tight circles. Garnet kept her eyes on the lord, watching his breathing quicken, his muscles tense, his mouth work. And then his eyes drifted from where Clover pleasured her, to meet her gaze.

The shock threw her over the edge in a few more rough strokes as she stared into his dark eyes.

Clover giggled during her throes, and she shoved the woman toward the redhead to cover the embarrassment of her too quick orgasm.

Losing her balance, Clover sprawled across the end of the couch near Sir Red. The lord helped her up, only to grip her thighs, spreading them, and shoving her down into his lap. He pushed her back against the sofa as he gripped the edge of the aged furniture. He slid into her, and his dark brown flickering gaze met Garnet's as he pounded into a mewling Clover.

Chapter 2: Sated, Not Satisfied

With a groan, he stumbled off the road toward a tree. Leaning his forearm against it, he rested his head against his arm as he freed himself with his other hand. The sweet release of piss had him uttering a different kind of sound, even as he had to shift his hips to the side to keep the sideways stream from hitting his boot. He watched the water trickle through the bark's cracks.

It was far too bright.

This time of night wasn't supposed to be this light.

"Couldn't have done that about one hundred yards back?"

Harry rolled his head, looking over his shoulder. He grinned, even as the lantern beam blinded him. "Slaaaaayth! Fedvich-ch-ch! Brothers, I... wait a moment." He returned his attention to the most important member of the party, shaking him dry before hiding him away. The redhead turned, arms wide, "Got a drink?"

"Think you've had enough, dragonbreath." Slayth said slowly, as if reprimanding a child. He held the lantern higher as he looked at the boy with raised brows.

Harry grunted, shielding his eyes from the light. "Put that down, will ya?"

Fedvich's dark chuckle filled the space between them. "Come on, let's get you to bed." He pulled Harry's arm over his shoulder, and leaned the drunk against him. They stumbled back onto the flat dirt gravel road, the gray stone walls of the training grounds reared high ahead of them.

"Gods, I almost had her." Harry groaned, thinking of the woman of his dreams waiting for him in bed.

"Her who?" Slayth asked, walking beside them on the wide road.

"You know, his precious gem Mistress." Fedvich shook his head. "How did you almost have her this time?"

"No, I really did! She wassh about to let me- I wants to taste her ss-ssso bad. She was right there. Garnet. But nooo, she took Clover. Not I." Harry wobbled, leaning heavily on Fedvich one moment and swaying away the next. "Me! Me! I coulda... why she not want me?"

"She's a fucking dominatrix, boy."

"Not a fucking one," Fedvich corrected Slayth. "Hence his drunken whining. A good dominatrix who knows how to keep the line. Like she's paid to do."

"I'd paysh to fuckker."

"Obviously," Fedvich muttered, then grunted as Harry swayed away and nearly toppled them both. "Slayth, make yourself useful."

"I got the lantern."

Fedvich shot the older man a glare, straightening Harry back onto his shoulder with a grunt. "For once being the second, you are not help."

Slayth corrected the sober one, "No help."

"Semantics."

"Ooh big word. So schmart." Harry poked Fedvich's cheek, a wide grin plastered on his face. When Slayth pushed open the door, he grinned, lifting both arms high. "We're home!"

Fedvich groaned at the force Harry used to celebrate, falling back with him as he grappled for a better hold on Harry's waist but came up lacking. Both redheads sprawled over the threshold of the training grounds, one laughing wildly, while the other cursed vehemently. The laughing one embraced the other, declaring that the stones covered in sand were their bed that evening.

"Get off!" Fedvich freed one hand, only to have to kick off a leg from around his, then another hand. "Slayth!"

"Lie in your bed; you made it." The elder chuckled, holding the lantern high to watch the drunken redhead mimic an octopus while the other fought off the tentacles with all his might.

"Fuuuuuuuuuuuuuuuck." Even his favorite word hurt. He opened his eyes, blinked, and took a moment to realize he was looking at the stone floor beneath his bed. His knuckles scraped against the floor before he found enough strength to lift his hand to hold his head.

The wood and floorboards squeaked and ground in complaint as he rolled fully onto his bed. He needed to refill the tick soon; he swore he could feel each and every leather band under it. Harry pulled his dagger free from his pillow as the door cracked against the stone like thunder and sat up in one fluid motion.

"Good morning, sunshine!" Fedvich screamed with head tossed back. "Drink?" he held out a pewter mug, "Or bucket?" he switched to holding the wood and iron vessel toward him.

Harry swallowed, but it didn't help the nausea. It rose in leaps. "I'll kill you after I throw up. Bucket!"

His dagger clattered to the floor as he gripped the vessel and loosed the contents of his stomach into it. After a few dry heaves, he set it on the ground and wiped his mouth off with the back of his hand. "Now... where were we?"

"Drink," Fedvich held out the mug again. "Then I'll beat the rest of the hangover out of you on the training grounds."

He snorted, taking the mug and gulping down the hair of the dog inside. "You will try, but you will not succeed."

Harry got dressed and met Fedvich on the grounds, he wished he hadn't accepted the challenge after a mere few hits. Still, as second, he couldn't let a little hangover get the best of him. Gritting his teeth, he slammed his sword hilt into the back of Fedvich's neck. Then he placed a boot on the defeated's shoulder when the other redhead tried to get up. "I win. Won. No more. Fuck you." He groaned, taking one step, then another away before letting his knees buckle. He fell into a sitting position, leaning on the wooden training weapon, and placing his throbbing forehead against it.

"We need to get ready, anyway." Fedvich said with a heavy sigh, still lying flat on his face. The puff of sand he caused with his own breath made him cough and sit up.

"What?" Harry stared at Fedvich.

"The hunt."

Sam Wicker

"Fuck me." Harry groaned, giving up what little hold he had on any strength and falling back, arms and legs spread wide as he closed his eyes against the asshole sun. "I can miss it."

"Not a chance. Reg said if he has to go, we *all* have to go." Fedvich sat up on his hands and knees. "Did you have to hit me so hard?" He asked, rubbing the back of his neck with a grimace.

"You wouldn't stay down!" Harry cried, giving Fedvich a gesture he reserved just for his comrades when they made him angry. He rolled, pushing himself back up. The only man he feared on this earth other than his father was one Regus Norvasos, or Duke Vicious. He wasn't about to face his wrath with a hangover.

After further bickering on the way to their barracks, and then Harry's maddening hunt for his good uniform amid the bloodstained and torn ones, he made himself ready. Running down the stairs while buttoning his jacket, Harry cursed as he sprinted across the grounds to the six men on their steeds. With a grin, Fedvich motioned to their fearless leader. The one who looked like a thundercloud about to strike him, and the one holding the reins to his horse.

Harry muttered an apology as he grabbed his reins and jumped onto the back of his horse. He was barely settled before The Seven urged their horses through the double doors to the rest of the grounds. Harry breathed a small sigh of relief when he met Virsin's gaze and saw her grin. "At least one person doesn't hate me."

She moved her horse into formation, right beside her husband at the head.

"We will have to rush, my love." Regus said, first looking at his wife before shooting a glare over his shoulder to Harry.

"I know. I wanted a good run. It's refreshing."

Harry cursed himself with each thundering hoofbeat between the duke's castle and the hunting forest three miles away. Forget what he thought; she hated him, too. He closed his eyes, leaning over the neck of his gelding, and murmuring, "Festus, keep me upright, old boy."

Heat. Sunlight. Scratchy uniforms. Men grumbling. Horses neighing and galloping. Perfect conditions for one Harrick Tearney. Glorious.

All those drinks because Mistress Garnet had denied him. Again. He would go back and try again with his Garnet tonight. Of all the doms there, she was his. Well, he wanted her to be his. Her voice, how her strikes hit, the weight of her boot on him, those sharpest of green eyes, and painted red lips behind the mask in a wicked smile struck all his desires true. Even how she made sure the flowers received an orgasm while under her command had Harry's heart galloping to her, desperate for acceptance.

He'd taken on every odd job, every bounty the king set forth, and saved all he could from the looting war. Harry swore he'd go back to his personal evil to steal from the dead if he needed more to gain her. Each lady there had a price, a debt, and he swore he'd set Garnet free after the first time he felt her whiplashes on his back. Until then, he wanted to give her as much pleasure as she gave him.

Last night, he'd nearly touched her.

Tonight, perhaps he finally would.

Chapter 3: Did I Ever Tell You About the Time I Killed My Brother?

Two Years before Survival of Bertran, 27 years ago
They shared the same eyes. He realized that again once she opened them wide as she screamed over the sizzle of her flesh burning under the brand. With their father's blood running through both their veins, and the red hair, that's where the similarities stopped. Unfortunately, that wasn't the case between him and the eldest.

He hated that he could be twins with the man slapping his cock against their sister's left breast. The men pinning her down on the table grinned lewdly as they waited for their comrade to heat the brand again. He wondered if they knew they'd die if they so much as hardened for her.

The sullying of a Tearney was for Tearney's alone.

He flexed, the tight leather bands over his biceps and forearms stretched, the old giving way as he spread the large cracks along the edges. Dearest brother should learn to keep his torture chamber better equipped. Still, the straps held him well enough for him to grow sick with the scene before him.

The seventh prince was pretty sure the first prince was about to make him rape the ninth princess.

Harrick was greater than that, though. He was going to free himself, then her, and kill the bastard prancing around half naked while their sister screamed. He flexed again; the leather snapped open on his left arm. Harry wrenched his right free, grabbed a whip from where it hung on the wall next to him and let it fly with a flick of his wrist.

The guard holding his sister's thigh screamed as his eye popped, spattering blood and tissue over the one across the table from him. His shriek melded with the female ones, echoing through the chamber. Harry slashed forward three more times in quick succession, blinding two of the filthy guards.

He glanced at his brother. The man was a grinning fool, watching the show. Just like their father, the firstborn reveled in other people's pain. Harry wondered how the eldest prince would enjoy experiencing his own torture. He was about to find out.

As the first guard held his hands to his eyes as if trying to stop the blood flow, Harry unsheathed the sword and used it to kill its own master by sinking it into the man's exposed side. He pushed through the hindrance of ribs, twisting to break the bones under his weight.

He utilized the wooden butt of the whip to smash the face of the guard rushing him. Harry yanked the sword free by kicking the limp body off it. He swung it into the neck of the third guard. The warm spray of blood splattered over his arms and chest. He spat, eyeing the fourth and last enemy, who still had his hands on his sister.

"Let her go."

"No, you'll kill me!" The guard cried, shuddering and making himself small behind her slender trembling shoulders.

"I won't. I'll let you live." Harry tried a smile and was pretty sure he failed at seeming nice when the guard paled even more. "Promise."

The guard glanced at the eldest Tearney, then back at the younger. He bolted for the closed double doors.

Harry lunged, swinging the sword hard with both hands, bending the unfortunate man in half as he swung the sword into his middle. "I didn't say how long I'd let you live." He growled, head-butting the man. When the guard fell, he planted the end of the blade into his thick neck and left it there. Striding away, he grabbed his sister's thin arm and yanked her behind him. With her pressed to his back, he felt her constant trembles, which emblazoned his anger. He turned, keeping her flush against him as he flipped the whip back and forth in his free hand. The lazy slaps of leather against the stone floor mixed with the shuffles of his and her feet.

"Bravo." The eldest smiled, clapping three times slowly as his hands shifted to claws.

"Show isn't over yet."

"No? You think you can kill me? Your own brother?"

"You lost the privilege of my caring for you the moment you began worshiping father." Harry tasted the bile at the mention of the man. He swallowed it down, circling them to stay squared up with the eldest as he moved around them. "Semir, have you thought about what you've been doing?" He couldn't concentrate enough to partially shift. He could kill her if he tried.

The first prince grinned, "I have, and I love every minute of it. It's a pity you won't join in on the fun. You and I, we are closer than you think. We have the exact same blood, same father, same mother. I know you want to."

Harrick shuddered, making his sister whimper behind him.

"Yarra is delicious. I branded her, but you can have a taste."

"Please don't. Please. Please. Please."

The sobs behind him wrecked his heart. No princess, no sister of his should fear her brothers this much. She shouldn't have to beg for common decency.

But that wasn't the kind of family they were born into.

Harry sighed, calming the storm of emotions within. "Yarra is under my protection now. I hate I couldn't get free in time to save her from your torture, or knew that you were..." Rage entered and tore through him again as he ground out, "That you were raping her sooner. I would have ended you long ago. Before you ever touched her."

She was still so young, too. Then again, Harrick felt decades older than his age. He'd grown up too fast, had to so he could survive.

In stopping the spiral of self-hate for not being enough, Harrick flicked the whip out. The end slashing a streak across Semir's hip wasn't what he'd planned. His brother was still nimble.

"I need you to go to that corner, Yarra, please?" Harry murmured, knowing he'd get them both killed if she slowed him. "Don't run away. I don't want anyone to grab you in your... state."

Her sobs racked her entire body, but she quickly slunk into the corner behind them. He turned just enough to see her press into the shadows, and then curl in on herself, hugging her knees to her chest to make herself as small as possible. Harrick let the rage erupt.

He spun around to face the eldest, the whip flying through the air, over and over again. Slashes appeared all over Semir's body, pinkening before oozing blood. He lunged toward his brother. Memories of them as boys, Harry not yet five and Semir barely ten, chasing frogs and salamanders by the single creek that ran through their country, filled his mind as he tackled Semir to the floor.

The stones scraped his arms and knees. He clambered up, slipping from the grip of Semir to wrap his hands around his brother's neck. He picked Semir's torso up; then slammed him down into the ground. A crack sounded.

Semir grinned, clawing at Harry's wrists and hands as he thrashed to be free. "You may not partake like I do, but you find joy in killing."

"I find joy in getting revenge. Of ridding the world of filth." Harry spat, struggling to keep his hold and his seat. He was glad of the extra training he tortured himself with. His weight exceeded Semir's, which proved his sole advantage.

He hissed as Semir's claws found purchase in his forearms and ripped his flesh. His hands grew slick with his own blood. Harry huffed, scrabbling to keep his chokehold, leaning forward to settle his weight to keep Semir from lifting him off. The whip caught his eye.

He shook off Semir's paw, yanking the whip toward him. As he was about to be thrown back, he slammed the butt of the whip into Semir's mouth. Putting his weight behind his hands again, he pressed his hand closed around the slick throat beneath him, while stuffing the whip's wooden handle with Semir's broken teeth, into the open maw. Red scales erupted over Semir's flesh, only to fade with the last ragged breaths.

He sneered down at his brother, growing limp under him, "One down, nine more to go."

Chapter 4: Perfumes and Horses

The fan was utterly useless in this heat. She took her brother's handkerchief from his hand, and dabbed at the sweat. Using the thin fan to lift her thick tresses off her neck, she dried the sweat there, too.

"Well, thank you, brother, for lending me your handkerchief even though you were in the midst of using it yourself. I, your dear sister, Addy, love you and will pay you back with a glass of lemonade. That I'm about to procure. Right now."

She met his green eyes, the only ones that matched hers in the family of five brothers, a mother, a father, and herself, Adeline, the only daughter. He, Percival, was the eldest, she was the youngest, and they were Viscount Pomm's children. "If I miss the shot, I shall pour the lemonade on your head, oh beloved brother mine."

"By all means, please do." Percy held his hands before him, his eyes wide.

Addy rolled her eyes before handing her reins to Percy and trotting off to the yellow ribboned tent that housed refreshments.

And all the ladies. And all their perfumes. And fannings.

She took a deep breath before stepping into the small enclosure, heading straight for the large cask that promised the sweetest lemonade beside a shard of ice that would mean relief from the dreadful sweltering. "Two lemonades, please." She smiled sweetly, trying not to breathe in.

She could feel her face begin to strain with her lungs, probably purpling. A far better color than the red of heat, was it not? Adeline cleared her throat, begging her body to hold out for a bit longer.

Only the ice was not chipping off as it should.

With a mental groan, she breathed. Perfume swam up into her nose and clung, making her eyes water. There were ten ladies clammed up under the shade of the tent with the ice being fanned toward them, and all of them had on a different scent.

The one with the foul rose smell sauntered to her, all pink dress and feathered fan. Adeline begged the ice to chip quicker. All she needed was to become more of an oddity by sneezing all over the rosed.

"My dear Adeline, why! you look positively male in those riding boots and trousers! How brave of you."

Addy would have laughed at the disdain dripping in the ruse of praise, but she hadn't the energy. "Why thank you, Miss Myra. It's a pleasure to ride during the hunt, a far better endeavor than marinating in florals."

At last, the two glasses of lemonade were ready, and she grabbed them up with a trousered curtsy. "Miss Myra." She curtsied again before rushing out to gasp in the fresh air.

Percy grinned and took his drink from her as soon as she had crossed a quarter of the field to him. "Choked?"

"Am I not blue?" Adeline asked after taking a long swig of the lemonade.

"Oh, dear gods, I'd be more than blue for another." Percy groaned, placing the cold glass against his forehead and rolling it.

Adeline drank the rest of her glass and wondered if she had time to get a second. Or should she not brave the stench again? "What are we waiting for?"

"The Duke Victory, of course." Percy said before taking a sip, his brow dripping with the condensation from his iced lemonade.

"He's dicking his wife, it'll be awhile." A man not much older than Percy said from the other side of him.

"Doxy's here?!" She swung her gaze around, looking for her other brother. She didn't get to see much of him these days, as he was bound to the Duke and had gone to serve instead of Percival.

"Probably watching him dick his wife." This one was from the pockmarked teen beside her.

Adeline tossed the empty glass to him, "Be a dear and return this for me." She batted her eyelashes at him, watched his eyes grow wide before he ran to the tent. Addy returned to scanning the crowd on either side of the narrow field. Only to realize it would be next to impossible to spot her shortest brother in the throng.

Thunder grew to the right, and she and the other hunt participants looked toward the single road leading to the grounds. Behind it, a plume of dust arose, and the thunder broke up into the sound of pounding hooves. A white stallion barreled around the refreshment tent, followed closely by seven others of varying colors. Including a fiery red long-legged steed, she recognized immediately. "Doxy and Starglow are here!"

"I swear you love your brother's horses more than you do us brothers." Percy muttered beside her. He handed off his glass to another, then bent to straighten the leather over his leg. In this weather, wearing pants, much less a long boot, irritated his leg more in the heat than ever.

Percy was the one unfortunate enough to inherit the family curse after their grandfather. Inflamed patches of skin dotted his body, the largest covering half of his calf on the left leg. Adeline and Doxy had smaller blotches, but they hardly became as painful as Percival's. With a bit of sunning, Addy could gain some control over the spread and itchiness. Doxy used lotions and sunned. Nothing seemed to aid in alleviating Percival's affliction, similar to their grandfather's suffering.

The massive man on the white steed slid off before the horse even stopped, and half ran before dropping to a long stride to reach the center of the field before the contestants. He held up his hands, "Lords and ladies, forgive my lateness! I am Duke Norvasos, or as some of you call me, Duke Victory. Ridiculous." The last word was uttered under his breath, but was still heard by many.

The man spoke to the crowd again as he looked to the left, then to the right, toward the rest of his party still mingling near the tents, his hands dropping to his sides. "I am here to start the hunt!"

Addy followed his gaze, grinning as Doxy tussled with a redheaded comrade before gaining whatever it was in the blue cloth. Her brother then ran toward the duke, holding out the cloth in both hands. Leather creaking and horses snorting broke into her observance of her brother.

A redhead. No, there were two. Addy felt her heart leap. What if her wayward thought from the other night was true and Sir Red was a member of The Seven?

She turned, helping Percy up onto his horse with a grunt, before settling into her own saddle. Her stallion's gray mane felt like silk in her fingers before she rubbed her hands down his arched neck. "I think we're finally ready, Sid." Sid was short for Obsidian. She couldn't help but name her stallion after her favorite Mistress, and mentor.

If she didn't look, they wouldn't look at her, right? She was being nonsensical. She couldn't even tell anything about them other than their build and red hair, surely, they wouldn't be able to pinpoint her out of the crowd.

"In these woods you will find baskets! In these baskets are shards of ice. Within the ice is a note with further instructions! Follow those, and you will gain your winnings once you return to the red tent. Are you all ready?" The duke bellowed before them; the pistol pulled from Doxy's hands pointed up to the sky at his shoulder.

Out of the corner of her eye, she observed some of the newcomers joining the field on their horses. She pondered if that was an unjust edge; the gallop warmed their steeds toward the hunt, or if it hurt them since her companions possessed fresh mounts. Addy looked over at Percy, "You're certain you don't want me to stay by your side? The baskets might be on the ground."

"Nonsense, find your prize, and I shall find mine." Percy smirked at her, looking as at home in the saddle as he was on a sofa. "You know I'll beat you, so I shall not have you endeavoring to hinder me."

Addy opened her mouth to say something, but the pistol released. Horses squealed, some reared, while she and Percy nudged their steeds forward. Soon, she and Sid outpaced Percy, and she grinned at Doxy as she passed him by. Then she was in the shade of the woods, Sid keeping his speed as he wove through trees. She waited until she heard few others in the surrounding forest before slowing down so she could begin her search.

"How hard can it be to spot a basket of ice?"

Sam Wicker

An hour later, Adeline thought herself a right fool for jinxing her chances not five minutes into the hunt. How difficult indeed. Sid was having fun, prancing through the forest. She let him have his head, for she figured the horse would have better luck than she.

She pulled her fan out of the breast pocket of her jacket. Fanning herself, she cursed the heat. "Why should I have this on?" Addy rolled her eyes at herself. No one was around. Surely, she could hear a man or horse come upon her before they saw her, too. Shrugging out of the thick jacket, she laid it across Sid's neck and then began plucking at her thin shirt to stop it from sticking to her.

A glance at the sun told her she was heading east, back toward the field. It was a different path from the one they'd come from, so she kept letting Sid pick the way as she lifted her blouse and fanned herself. No one was around. Not a soul.

"My lady, you must be careful, you never know who you might come across in the wilds."

She froze on top of her horse, then dropped her shirt, and nearly fell off as Sid took a little jump across a fallen branch. Grappling for a hold, she cursed her luck. There was a grunt behind her, hands on her hips, and a warmth enveloped her while making her clothes stick against her back again.

Then she saw the bright blue sky peeking between the thick green foliage as Obsidian reared with a shriek.

Air escaped her as she hit, her fall cushioned by whatever or whoever had a hold of her. In a second, she flipped her fan, hitting the thing behind her with all the force she could muster until she filled her lungs with a gasp. Sitting up, she tried to gain her feet, only to be held still by wide hands on her hips.

"Easy, I say!"

Had he been talking this whole time? Addy whirled, looking down at her captor. "Easy? Easy, you say? What were you thinking, jumping on the back of my horse?!"

"Of saving you, my lady." Sharp eyes slashed into hers, "You were falling from your saddle."

"Then let me fall!" She smacked him across the chest with her fan, "And unhand me!"

He raised his arms, then clasped his fingers together to lace them behind his head. His boots crossed at the ankles under her, making her shift from one side to the other in her seat upon him. Thick thighs. Muscles. Probably one of the warriors from the duke's legendary regiment. Did he train her brother? Did he like Doxy? Was Doxy a good person to have in the group?

"Do you know Doxy? Is he doing well?" She turned, straddling his abdomen as she peered down into his brown eyes. "Did I hurt you?" She patted his chest. A hard chest. He had red hair.

Red hair. Fit. But... it wasn't the same. Was it?

Her heart bolted down into her stomach.

No. No. No.

"My lady, I know Doxy well. How do you know him?"

The voice was entirely different. Not him. Not the man who knew her secret best. She breathed a sigh of relief and then smiled as Sid nudged her shoulder with his soft nose. Patting her horse's cheek, she answered the redhead under her, "I'm his sister, Addy."

"Ah, I see." He cleared his throat, "Well, my lady, considering you are a sister to one of my companions, I should suggest you get back on your horse instead of continuing to straddle me. I'm not complaining, mind you, but it might seem a bit... unlady-like."

Her face heated to twice its original temperature, and she shot up. "Forgive me!" She cried, gathering Sid's reins after he startled at her sudden movements.

"I shall not, for there is nothing to forgive." He grinned, still lying on the ground as if it were his bed. "And as for dear Doxy, he is doing well. Not a hair on his head has been harmed. Much."

There was a mischievous glint about his features as he spoke.

"And you are, sir?" Addy looked around, stepping over the man and around her horse. Her jacket had to be somewhere. She should return to being a proper lady before... well, before anyone else saw her state.

"Fedvich, my lady Pomm, at your service."

"Are you not partaking in the hunt?" At the base of a large pine, she spotted her jacket. Rushing over to it, she brushed the pine needles and dirt off it before shoving her arms through the holes and buttoning it up quickly.

"My job, along with the other six, is to make sure nothing untoward happens."

Addy snorted, standing back up to regard him, "Like jumping on a lady?"

Fedvich sat up, a grin on his face as he leaned on one hand, "My lady, if I had jumped you, you and I both would be bare to the earth and crying to the sky."

"An unlikely scenario, seeing as how no man has made me stir, sir." She snapped out. Well, that wasn't lady-like. She shouldn't know what he meant, should she? If she were a normal lady? "I must go." She shot up into the saddle and turned Sid's rear toward Fedvich so he wouldn't witness her red face. "Good day."

Sid leapt forward, trotting away at a nice pace. "Gods of fuck, what am I doing?" Addy asked herself with a groan.

When she raised her head, stars winked in her vision as her forehead smacked into something hard. Whimpering and rubbing her new pump knot, she twisted in her saddle to see what she had hit while stopping Sid. There hanging on a low oak branch with ribbons tied all around was a basket.

Chapter 5: Warrior Dreams of Garnet Mistress

Wet under his tongue, a Garnet crying his name, and a slash against his back would set any day straight. He was about to dream of such things when his feet were kicked off the chair before him, and he nearly fell out of the seat he was settled in. He pulled the handkerchief off his face. Some flirty miss had embroidered the handkerchief with roses and given it to him in the refreshment tent. His glare quickly turned into a smile, "Greetings, my very vicious but delightful duke, sir."

"Why are you hungover, and why aren't you fulfilling your duties?"

That's how it was going to be. He watched the arms that could break him in half fold over the broad chest. "First question, I'm a fool. Second is a simple answer: I'm hungover." So much for escaping into a quiet place early. Regus hadn't finished his little speech when Harry happened upon his oasis and the enchanting lady washed in rose perfume.

Harry hit his knees when those dark brows twitched toward the hairline, "I beg of you, Duke! Spare me!"

He glanced behind Regus, suppressing his smile as public attention shifted. Some ladies gasped, their fans fluttering and eyes wide over the laced edges. He returned to staring up Duke Vicious' nose. Doxy needed to trim those things. Thick as an evergreen forest. He then began to smile, fluttering his eyelashes, similar to how a prostitute would while kneeling before someone of Regus' stature.

"Get your ass up and in that chair," Regus growled, noting the looks they were getting with a few flicks of his dark gaze.

"Yes, sir, Duke, sir. Happily." Harry nodded, pushing himself up and back into the chair he'd vacated. He frowned when

Regus dropped into the seat he'd been using to recline. So much for sleeping it off.

"Who took your quadrant?"

"Fedvich." Harry scanned the room for another footrest.

"Who gave you this?" Regus snatched the handkerchief dangling loosely from Harry's fingers.

"Some lady in rose." Harry lifted a shoulder, eyeing an empty chair just outside the tent. When he caught Reg's look out of the corner of his eye, he huffed, "Don't expect me to remember all the names of the ladies here. This is the first time I've met most of them. Your wife doesn't have enough time off your dick to hold gatherings of these ladies."

"Not to mention you only desire an unobtainable one these days." Regus added, dropping the handkerchief in Harry's hand. He leaned back, checking the box on the table in front of him. "No one has returned yet?"

"It's barely been half an hour, give the little lords time." Harry spotted an elderly lord hobbling toward the tent. He sighed as the elder occupied the chair that he'd planned to steal. "She's not so unobtainable," Harry let his grumpiness win and slumped.

"Have you even asked after her debt?" Regus picked up the small box and twirled it in his hands.

"The Madame has an odd way of wording things. The first time she said I'd never afford a life with her, the next time it was that I'd be in her debt for life, and then this last one was a sigh and shutting the door in my face."

"Then you'd best find yourself a lady. Virsin will invite her friends over. One day."

The way Regus' lips twisted made Harry doubt the duke's words. "Virsin has no friends."

The incredulous look would have garnered more than a few laughs if it wasn't followed by, "She does! She is perfection. How could she not have friends?"

Harry placed a hand on Regus' shoulder, "Perfection does not friends make." He let those words sink in before hitting his point home, "Look at me, all I have are The Seven, and I'm perfection."

Regus' expression didn't put Harry at ease. Had he worded it wrong?

"Harrick, you're like a brother to me, but I need to tell you a secret."

"Oh?"

"You're not perfect."

He clutched his chest, "It burns. Pain, such pain!" Falling back against his chair, he felt it give a little. Was the poor piece of furniture about to break under him?

"If Fedvich took your quadrant, who is watching out for Doxy's little sister?" Regus turned quickly toward the woods.

"She needs looking after?" Harry slowly straightened in the chair, barely breathing. "Who wants to watch after some skinny kid? She'll be fine."

"Fedvich volunteered for it. And I think she's grown."

Harry snorted, knowing the reason behind that all too well. While he whined about Garnet, Fedvich would complain about how clueless Doxy was. He felt sorry for the kid when realization hit him and Fedvich had his way. He doubted he'd see the two of them for weeks, much like the duke in front of him when he finally gave in to his duchess. Not that he would expect anything less. Once he bought Garnet and won her heart, he would never leave her.

A crack sounded, and Harry cursed before he dropped to the ground.

"What is it with you and chairs?"

"This is the only one *you* haven't broken! Ask yourself that question!" Harry glared up at Regus. "May I be dismissed? I have a hangover to get rid of before I go woo my love tonight."

"If I must smell all this perfume and sit in this sweltering tent, so do you." Reg grinned, "Besides, I have my own woman, and she lets me have all I want."

"Ass." Harry nodded, "You are an ass." He stood, brushing himself off. "Very well, then. I'll go find the littlest Pomm and kiss her scrapes so Doxy can relax."

"Take your quadrant and Doxy will actually rest easy knowing his sister won't be pawed at."

Harry waved at his commander over his shoulder. He was going to find a nice thick tree with a flat branch and sleep. He was pretty sure Regus knew his plan, too.

That limb proved simple to locate, possessing even a pleasant breeze originating from the lake. Sleep was not accomplished. For once he closed his eyes, something crashed through the woods and stopped beneath his bed. Harry looked up at the sky and cursed the gods. He then turned his gaze downward and saw a blond man sitting astride a pretty blond horse. Matching set, Harry thought to himself.

A basket already rested within his lap, plus one suspended from the rear of his saddle. One was wet from the remnants of the clue, while the other was pristine and held a small stone cushioned in blue velvet. The horseman looked all around, the animal pawing the ground impatiently.

Lost.

Harry debated letting the man go, but when he turned his steed in the wrong direction, he groaned. He had a job to do. "Sir."

The man jumped, horse balking with him, drawing him directly under Harry's branch, but the blond eventually looked up at him. The top of the man's head was right at his hip, any closer and he could sit on him. Not that he would ever do that, to a strange man.

Green eyes.

Familiar green eyes.

Harry's heart beat faster in his chest as he stared down into them. The lips had a different shape. His heart dropped and dropped further when he heard the voice.

"Hello?"

Idiot. He was an idiot. His Garnet didn't hold a hint of masculinity in her voice. "You're going the wrong way." Harry pointed to his right.

"Oh, thank you..."

"Harrick or Harry." He answered with a lift of his shoulder. He leaned forward, peering closely at those eyes that were uncannily like his beloved's. "You've got pretty eyes."

The blond leaned back, drawing the reins up tight in his gloved hands. "Thanks."

"Share them with anyone?"

"Addy."

"Addy?"

"My little sist- why does it matter?"

Harry ground his teeth; there was no way Garnet was a lord's sister. She was in debt. No lord at this hunt had such a disgrace to their name. So, he smiled widely, "I like green eyes. Always said I'd marry a green-eyed girl."

The man scoffed, "Addy is not so easy to handle, green eyes or not. And neither am I, and I am protective, as are my other brothers."

"Little do you know, I rise to challenges. Your name, sir?" Harry was invested now. He'd have the entire family eating out of his hand before the fortnight was out.

"Pomm. Percival Pomm."

Fuck. That was a bit too much of a challenge. Although... Doxy's face when Harry strolled around with his little sister on his arm... worth it. Worth every duel. All five of them.

"Well, Percival Pomm, I'm Harrick Tearney. Little Doxy knows me deeply. Pleased to make your acquaintance. I look forward to getting to know you, and little Addy, much better."

Chapter 6: Iced Dicks

Whoever had tied the knots in the ribbons was a professional. If she hadn't the patience her hobby demanded her to have, she would have slashed the basket to bits. The wicker was soaked through, and so was her jacket by the time she removed the thing from the limb. Looking inside, she grabbed the ice shard.

She stared at it.

"Quite a shape. Surely, they didn't carve them like this?" She shook her head and laughed at herself for her ridiculous thought. She broke the knob off the top and tugged the furled note free of the central tunnel in the ice shard.

"To complete your task and gain honor, find the rainbow stone in the crystal waters. East and North, old lady willow will guide you." Addy read to Sid, as if her horse would help her.

She looked toward the northeast. "Isn't there a lake... ah yes. In the middle." The map they had provided the hunters was etched in her mind. Addy thought through her meandering trek through the forest, and how much she had circled back on Sid. It shouldn't be too far, if her calculations were correct.

"Wonder if Percy has completed this already?" She mused to herself, the redhead forgotten. She urged Sid forward, heading in the direction she thought the lake might be. Soon, she heard the bubbling of water rushing. Afterwards Sid walked to the side of the sole river in the forest.

She glanced up, then down, and Adeline noticed the shore where the river entered. "Perfect." The sun was high above; she turned Sid to skirt the edge of the lake as she scanned for a willow tree. Not too far ahead, the long limbs of a monstrous willow brushed the lake's surface. Between her and it was a rocky beach, and uneven terrain.

Sliding off Sid, she patted his neck and let him nip at the grass.

With her arms extended, she began the slippery trek along the stones and slanted bank. A few times she thought she would fall into the lake, or onto the rounded moss-covered rocks, but somehow, she kept her footing. Mostly. Sure, she caught herself once or twice. Before she fell on her ass and cried like a toddler because she swore she broke something.

Where was Fedvich to break her fall?

Stubbornness was a family trait that she was proud of. She hobbled the rest of the way to the willow trunk. Etched into the bark were four arrows. Addy stared at them, holding a hand to her ass and trying not to whimper again. Two were blue, one red, and one yellow.

"Rainbow stone," she murmured to herself, willing the arrows to tell her what she needed instead of having to guess. She wasn't very fond of puzzles.

Red was the first color in the rainbow. Red was the color of her infatuation's hair. She sighed, deciding to go with the red arrow, which pointed to the right of the tree. The old willow's roots were as slippery as the rocks. After the first slip and pain shooting up and down from her ass, she hugged the trunk. Reaching the other side, she walked along the beach, carefully picking her way between roots and rocks and patches of slime.

Addy stepped on it before she registered it was different. A red rock pressed in between moss-covered ones under a raised root. Bending with more than a few curses, she picked the painted stone up, careful not to turn it lest there be another arrow.

There was. Pointing to the lake. Addy sighed, tossing the clue over her shoulder. She didn't think she could straighten back up; pretty sure she should remain squatting for the rest of her life. If she called the names of Fedvich or Doxy thrice, would it summon them? It wouldn't hurt to try.

"Doxy. Doxy. Doxy." She waited a few beats. Addy laughed at herself, and tried again, "Fedvich. Fedvich. Fedvich."

Nothing.

She huffed a breath, and half walked, half slid and scooted her way to the lake's edge. Maybe the next clue would be right in front of her face. Addy admired the clarity of the water for a heartbeat before she noticed a striped stone. In the depths. She would need to swim, or wade, to reach it.

Sam Wicker

"Fucking perfect." She muttered to herself, shrugging out of her jacket while trying to remain squatting.

That put her back on her ass quicker than she imagined. Hissing through her teeth, she flung her coat toward her horse with another curse. Angry enough at the pain, she jerked her boots off, and they followed the jacket. Shimmying out of her pants, she growled through the smarting before throwing them, too.

"Bastard Duke. Idiot Fedvich. Damnable hunt!" She crouched, stepping into the lake with a hiss. "Of course this is the only blessed thing that's cold!" Other than the ice... phallus. Had they carved it like that, truly?

With her breath hitching, she waded further into the water, then kicked off. Cold and pain. Pain and cold. Breathe. Stone. Why was she doing this?

"Oh, I hope Percy found an easy challenge." She wished to the lake, before looking down to see if the tiny painted rainbow appeared under her yet. Yes. She smiled and sank herself. She felt for the stone, her fingers closing around it right as her lungs began burning.

Up again, and she could breathe.

"You called?"

"Fu-" She spluttered, staring at the man on the bank. He held her boots in one hand, her pants and jacket in the other, and a grin on his lips.

"There was a basket where you tried to ride me, if you'd taken your eyes off me long enough to look around. That challenge was not as..." He licked his lips, his eyes on her as if he could see through the... he could!

"Cold." He ended his taunt, his smirk returned.

"Turn around, sir!"

"Why?"

She wanted to throw something at him. All she had was water and... she smirked. "Turn around, or I'll make your brains come out of your ears."

"Well, that's a nasty visual." Fedvich's brows rose, "And how will you do that?"

"Like this!" She rose from the water, rearing her arm back and then slinging it forward. She loosed the stone and smiled as it flew true.

Fedvich's knees buckled as his head slung back with the force of her throw. He toppled, like a tree felled. He was still.

Adeline swam quickly to reach the slippery shore and crawled toward her clothes clutched in the knight's hands. "Ow. Ouch. Fuck. Ow." She cursed under her breath with each step. The words erupted more vehemently as she tugged her pants on over wet legs.

"Would it have been better if I had worn these in?" She yanked and pulled, staring down at the long rip along the inside seam after that dreadful noise swallowed out the lake's gentle laps. The thick flakes of her disease peeking from the crack. "Oh, for gods fucking." She jumped, pulling as hard as she could to get her trousers over her thighs and rear, ignoring the extra rip, and the sharp pains. She shucked her shirt and yanked on her still-damp jacket, but at least it was thicker, and not as cold. Buttoning the fabric closed about her, she stood over the redhead.

It was uncanny to have two long-haired redheads in sight within the span of two days, was it not?

His chest rose and fell, and she nodded. He was alive. She eyed her boots, stepping gingerly over him to grab them from his hands. If these weren't her favorites, she would have left them. Grunting in the effort to pull her leg back over his bulk, she took a few steadying breaths. She was still half bent forward, finding the position eased the pain.

Sid whickered nearby.

"Fuck."

"Well... if you insist..." Fedvich muttered with a groan, his hand rising to touch the knot forming between his eyes. He looked at his fingertips as if expecting to see blood, when he didn't, he touched the bump again and hissed as he sat up on one elbow. His gaze swept up and down her, "Why are you standing like that?"

"My ass is broken."

He snorted only to sober when she glared at him. "Broken ass, got it." He cleared his throat. With a whimper and groan, he pushed himself to his feet, swaying slightly as he straightened. "Might have a broken rear, but you have one hellish arm."

"Doxy kept stealing my slingshot, so I learned how to do without one." She smiled a little at the memories before straightening herself. "Oh, I can't do this. Go on without me. I'll just live here."

Fedvich laughed, "Come on." He stooped to grab the rainbow stone and leaned dangerously to one side, then the other when he stood back up. The redhead grunted, shaking his head slightly, before closing the distance between them and sliding the rock into her jacket pocket. He looked down at her feet, where her shirt was, "You fond of that?"

"Not particularly."

"Good." He moved to stand in front of her, facing away, and held his arms above his hips, hands bent toward her and open. "Get on."

She stared at his hands, trailing her gaze up his back to give herself time to think. He was all lean muscle, she felt it when she landed on him, but he wasn't that strong. "Let me get my boots on."

"No need, I'll be carrying you." Fedvich said, looking at her over his shoulder.

The knot was turning a rather comical purple and would soon make his brows dip down. She decided not to comment on that observation. Being carried seemed like the better option between walking, riding, and crawling. It was unfortunate that it wasn't a day they were able to shift. She could use the warmth of her scales. Addy looked down at her pants, seeing the rip was indeed showing off her flaking skin on her right leg. She sighed.

"Boots first."

Fedvich exhaled, burdened as if she were his torment. "Fine."

He turned, his brows rose. At least the part not affected by the bump. "Get to it, then."

"I... can't."

"Broken ass?"

She nodded, "Broken ass."

"Well, let's do this." He bent, scooping her up in his arms. Straightening, he wove back and forth as he squeezed his eyes shut. "I can walk us back while you put your boots on, I count that as a victory."

Adeline bit the inside of her cheek to keep from screaming. How dare he manhandle her. "Why did you come and not Doxy?"

"Do you come when your name is said three times?" Fedvich asked, picking his way across the stones carefully to the steep bank.

"No, I'm not... oh." She rolled her eyes at herself.

"Witchkin, you can say it." Fedvich scaled the embankment, and turned toward her horse. "Will he follow?"

"He will." Addy clicked her tongue, "Come on, Sid, come along."

"You still have the basket." Fedvich observed out loud with a slight grin. "Grab the ice." He said when Sid came near.

Addy did as she was told and held the two pieces in her hands.

"Long one for your ass, and the small one for my head. Letting you down." He claimed before he dropped her to her feet. "Loosen your pants." He said, his fingers sliding into the band.

"Wait! What are you doing?"

Fedvich paused, leaning over her to meet her gaze as she turned to look up at him, "Your ass hurts, right? That's curved, should fit nicely."

Addy looked up at the canopy, pressing her lips tight together to keep the curses and thoughts behind them.

"It's not like we're putting it *in* there." Fedvich said, and she heard the chuckle in his tone.

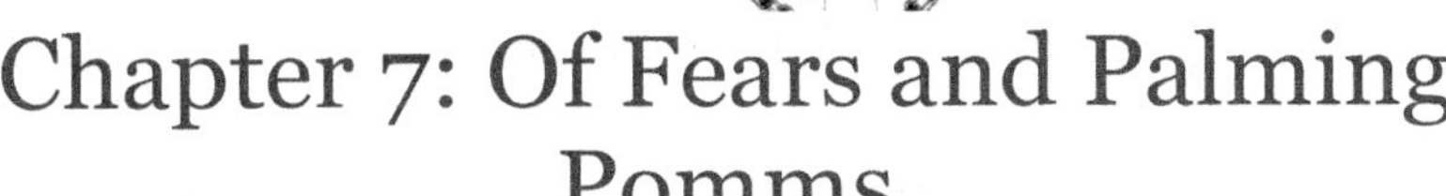

Chapter 7: Of Fears and Palming Pomms

"Since you are insisting on following me, why green eyes?"

Harry bought himself a moment by humming. He couldn't very well tell someone he was trying to woo about his mistress. "My first love was a girl with green eyes." He watched as Percival reached into the top of his boot and scratched. That made the tenth time. "Do you need an ointment? Something bite you?"

Percy's face burst into red as his hand jerked back to his reins. "No, nothing like that."

Harry waited a beat. Then another. Was that all he was going to receive? He rolled his eyes, letting the horse get ahead of him a little. He swept his gaze over Percival's form. Slight slouch, that made for a comfortable ride, nothing telling about that. Thin. Wasn't Percival the eldest? Doxy was not a big man by any means, but he was thicker than that. A sign of sickness, a long-lasting one. Disease.

The Pomms were dragonkin like him. Therefore, there weren't that many diseases or infections they couldn't heal from. An itch, constant. Harry grimaced, knowing what it was once he thought it through. The hereditary skin disease. Once a dragonkin remained in one form or another for too long, a disease infected the flesh of both. In dragon form, their scales were weaker in the patches of afflicted areas if they didn't disintegrate completely. Never to grow back. In human form, patches of dry skin grew constantly and flaked off, sometimes causing bleeding and further infection if severe.

If a dragonkin fell under the spell of keeping to one form over another for too long, their descendants could inherit the disease. Sometimes it was every offspring; other times it was one or two here or there. The severity also fluctuated.

He recalled Doxy mentioning something inherited from his grandfather. Harry had brushed it off as old money, as most lords inherited their fortunes. It appeared that wealth and titles were not the sole inheritance passed down amongst the Pomms.

It also explained why Percival wasn't with them, but Doxy was.

"Percival, it's nothing to be ashamed of." He watched the expression grow from embarrassed to shocked, back to red. "I'm glad you have fun with things like this. I had a friend who allowed the itch to take over his life. He never left home. Don't let that happen to you."

Though brief, a laugh arose, interrupting the quiet as they moved through the wooded area. Percival said, "There is no chance my family would allow me to sleep in, much less stay housebound."

Harry remembered why they had added Doxy to The Seven so quickly. The kid had spunk and speed. Spunk and speed were both necessary to wake their duke and survive. Doxy also had a streak of stubbornness a mile wide and a sense of duty that rivaled Regus'. "I can see that."

Percival looked down at him, "Is my brother well liked? Does he behave?"

"Oh, he's liked all right. Downright loved. He's the only one quick enough to dance out of Regus' reach and can get away with Virsin hugging him." Harry shook his head with a chuckle, "He's an excellent addition, and I promise he is well guided and protected."

"I shall pass that on to our parents. I'm sure it will please them." Percival stated, looking ahead and ducking a low limb.

Harry paused, something happening deeper in the trees to his right. He wasn't sure what drew his attention, but soon he made out a long, drawn-out scream. The sound of a large beast or person accompanied it, crashing through the underbrush and running over the leaf litter. He held out a hand, stilling the horse and pushing them back to the edge of the tiny clearing. Stepping up to the edge of the shadows created by the trees above them, Harry made sure he would be between whatever was coming and Percy.

Why didn't he have his sword?

Sam Wicker

Oh, he was in his dress uniform, the only one without blood on it. Besides, there was nothing dangerous in these woods. Abundant growth created habitats for tiny birds plus beasts, with no sizable predators present, thus forming a paradise suitable for dainty lords.

Right.

"It sounds..." Percival began.

The bush to the left and in front of Harry burst open, letting a blur of limbs in tan pants and a blue jacket that matched Harry's out into the oval clearing. A constant scream poured from the red-faced soldier. He didn't even notice Harry, the horse, or its rider along the edge. The shrub hugging trees across the way quickly took the man back into the depths of the woods. Shrieks continued after him, fading with distance.

Harry cursed, turning to look back toward where his comrade had come from.

"That was Doxy, right?" Percy asked, a higher pitch to his voice.

"It was."

"Right." Percival's swallow was audible over the fading scream of his brother.

Whatever Doxy was running from had to be ferocious. The boy could face down Duke Regus Norvasos, aka Duke Vicious, and not bat an eye. Much. Why wasn't there a sound of this beast chasing Doxy reaching them yet?

A furball flew from the bush, took two leaps across the leaf litter in front of them, then followed Doxy into the far greenery.

Harry blinked, sure he'd missed something. He glanced back toward the right, where Doxy had first appeared. Nothing else was coming, that he could tell. He looked back at Percival, staring as the man was folded in half on top of his horse, shaking erratically. "You all right?"

"A... it's a-a-a squirrel." Percy forced through bouts of silent laughter.

"A squirrel." Harry repeated, trying to make sense of what he'd witnessed.

"Umhm." Percy guffawed, nearly falling off his steed.

Harry put a hand in the man's waistband, holding him steady as the laughs kept flowing. "Was it rabid?"

"No!" Percy cried, giving up and lying on his horse's neck, holding his sides with both hands. "He's... so scared... of them!"

He joined Percy, tears flowing from his eyes as he sat down to keep from falling down. "You... You have to be joking..."

"No. No! I'm not!" Percy sniffled, then laughed so hard he hiccupped.

Harry joined in until he hurt, then slowly got himself up and dusted off. He chuckled as he claimed, "I'm bound to catch every squirrel in this kingdom."

Percival's eyes glinted, his lips turning up in a grin of wickedness, "We have one hundred and three already."

Another bout of laughter broke him, "The Duke's household shall meet your challenge and raise you another hundred, for the torture of dear Doxy."

Had Doxy's misfortune won Percival over for him? Indeed, Harry thought it did. Two down and five more Pomms to go. "Should we rescue him?"

"Leave him. He needs to build his character."

Harry grinned up at Percy, knowing right then he'd welcome Percy at his table of shenanigans any day. "And his stamina."

Chapter 8: Ass Ice Cocks

After a lot of breaks because Addy felt guilty for Fedvich carrying her, they reached where the forest thinned. "You tell anyone about this..." Addy warned, tugging on the loose silken red strands before playing with them. How was his hair so soft?

"You tell anyone about felling me with one little rock and I will end up telling the world about your ass ice cock." Fedvich tossed back at her, hitching her up higher on his back.

Good one. Ass Ice Cock. "What are your powers, anyway?" She hadn't asked him yet. She meant to figure it out on her own, but curiosity was getting the better of her.

"Speed."

"Oh. That's impressive."

"Except when you let a rock hit you in the forehead instead of dodging it."

Addy giggled, resting her cheek on her arm that was loosely around his shoulders and neck. "Is that how you jumped on Sid before I even noticed you there?"

"It is. Doxy asked me to watch out for you if I saw you. Told all of us," Fedvich added, glancing over to observe Sid eating grass to their left. "Best be glad it was me who found you."

"Why?" Addy had heard little about Doxy's companions. The regular gossip, of course, and the few things Doxy divulged in stories once he was permitted to visit completed her scant knowledge.

"Unlike the others, I have a single-minded endeavor at the moment. And this time I happen to be interested in another Pomm." The eye he turned on her held a hint of metallic sheen.

"Hm," Addy considered his words. "You'll have to put his dick in your mouth before he accepts you're after him." She was pretty sure he meant Doxy, but any of her brothers were rather difficult to pin down in the romance department.

Fedvich laughed, "You definitely have four brothers."

If he only knew. She saw the clearing through the trees and sat up to rest her hands on his shoulders. "I should get down."

"That would be best." Fedvich agreed, stopping and gathering her wrists in his hands to help her slide down his back to gain her feet gently. He then touched the knot on his forehead and whispered with a breathy curse. "Need me to pull the ice out?" He asked, turning to her.

She shook her head, running her hand over her rear again just to make sure. "It melted, and the rest of my pants are wet or damp. It won't matter much." Addy had underestimated him; he wasn't out of breath carrying her that far through the forest. Doxy's companions were oddly terrifying.

Fedvich gave her a nod, then tapped her pocket with the stone, "Don't forget to claim your prize." He grinned and leaned toward her, "If I might make a suggestion... go for yellow or green. Definitely not red, orange, or indigo. Or play it exceptionally safe and choose violet or blue." He stepped aside, motioning for her to go ahead of him through the trees and into the field.

Once in the sunlight, she blinked back the burning brightness. When she turned, he was gone. "Yellow or green or blue or violet. Right."

Surveying the field, she noticed a majority of rivals had already arrived. She wondered how many got to claim a prize or if some had given up. She took the stone out of her pocket, running her thumb over the smooth paint as she made her way to the tent, Sid following her close behind.

Each step was agony.

"Addy?"

She looked up, searching for the owner of the familiar voice, and smiled. "You made it?"

Percy nodded as he limped toward her, a grin flashing his straight teeth and making his eyes gleam. "Got my prize." He held up his wrist, showing off a thick band of intricately woven cords of blue, red, and black. "And a new friend, I think. He went back into the woods after delivering me to the field. I hope Doxy won't find him and beat him for not saving him from the squirrels."

"What is it?" Addy's brows rose to her hairline as Percy revealed Doxy's attack. "I'm glad you met a new friend." She shook her head after thinking for a moment, "I think Doxy is the weakest of The Seven, so your friend should be fine."

"A witchkin's protection band. I think you're right."

"Oh! That's useful." Addy studied it, prodding at a few of the threads. It was soft to the touch, too.

"I think I might give it to Doxy," Percy added, then bent to catch her eye, "You look pale. And wet. You alright?"

"I broke my rear." Addy admitted with a roll of her eyes. "And he needs all the protection he can get, especially from little furry things."

Percival nodded slowly, championing through his need to chuckle with barely a twitch of his lips, "That's terrible."

She punched his shoulder, "Do not."

"I'm not!" Percy cried, holding up a hand while the other rubbed his upper arm. He glanced around, "Which one of these unfortunate sops are we going to convince to rub ointment on it, though?"

Adeline shook her head, "I told you not to make fun of me."

"Honestly, I'm not."

"Sure. Sure." Addy shot a glare his way, then continued toward the tent, "I have my own prize to claim."

"I'll search for a pair of fine hands." Percy chuckled, holding his own up as he turned and walked the opposite direction. He grabbed Sid's reins as he went, the gray stallion following gladly.

"Of all the brothers, I'm saddled with the eldest during the hunt." Adeline muttered to herself, walking as fast as she dared, failing to ignore the pain with each step. "Red, blue, violet, yellow." She didn't think that was right all of a sudden. Oh no, Percy distracted her too much.

Entering the tent, thankfully devoid of ladies as they were mingling with the single men on the field, she handed her small rainbowed rock to the Duke behind the table after bowing awkwardly.

He glanced at the stone in his hand before dropping it in a box, "Name?"

"Adeline Pomm."

"Doxy's little sister," the duke's scar added to the depth of his smirk. "Pick a color of the rainbow."

Red was her favorite, but she was pretty sure she was not supposed to choose that hue. Gods, why couldn't she remember things for longer than a few moments? "Violet."

"Well done. You earned tea with Duchess Norvasos, my wife. She will be in touch soon with an invitation."

Adeline bit back the giddiness, excitement swelling in her breast. Tea with the Duchess Victory! "What were the other colors, if I may ask?"

The Duke lifted the stone from the box of returned prizes, turning it in his fingers, "Red was a date with Harry, Orange was Fedvich, yellow is a meal with Bertran, green Slayth and his massive compilation of children, blue is an excursion with your dear brother. I'm sure you're glad you didn't choose that. Indigo was a dinner with yours truly, and violet is the one you chose. I believe it to be the best choice."

She bowed, grimacing through the pain when she dropped her head, "I believe you to be correct, Duke Norvasos. I look forward to having tea with the Duchess."

"Dismissed. Get your wound checked, Miss Pomm."

She blinked, then smiled a little to herself, "Yes, sir."

Turning back, she recrossed the field to where she saw Sid tied to a bench in front of their family tent. Her father was brushing him down in long strokes of the soft brush. As she neared, she met his gaze when he looked up. "Father."

"I heard you're hurt." His concerned stare trailed over her, "Get in there."

"Yes, sir." Addy nodded, passing through the narrow opening. The heat seemed caught in place under the canopy, and she had to stop to learn how to breathe again.

"Why are you missing a shirt?" Doxy asked, sitting up straight beside the table in the middle of the tent.

Addy grinned, "Nice to see you, too."

"I know, but answer me." Doxy rose, hugging his sister, then guiding her to a chair he pulled out for her.

"I was ravished by one of your friends you told to keep watch over me. So impatient, he ripped it."

Sam Wicker

Doxy's face burned bright red as his fists clenched at his side. Then he sucked in a breath through tight lips before letting it out his nose, "Comical."

Addy widened her eyes, trying to find a way to sit that caused the least discomfort. "Truth."

"It is not!" Doxy cried, then paused to stare her down, "Is it?"

She giggled, "No, it isn't."

Doxy slumped in his chair with a sigh of relief, "Good."

"Think you could best any of them if they took my honor?"

"Gods no." Doxy groaned, running a hand over his face, "I'd die before I could even say my greetings."

"Why would you greet someone you were dueling?"

Doxy lifted a shoulder, "Manners?"

Addy snorted, then laughed as Doxy grinned. "Fedvich helped me when I fell. Twice. You should help me think of something to send him in appreciation." She smiled a little to herself, "Or make him a meal yourself. You still make that loaded bowl thing, right?"

"Pot pie?" Doxy rolled his eyes at her, "Yes, I will make him a pot pie, dearest sister."

She wasn't sure who would owe whom by the end of Fedvich getting his pie. Addy turned her head to watch Percival enter the tent, two ladies entering behind him. She made a face, dreading what was to come as much as keeping the pain.

"Dox, out. They need to rub Addy's butt."

Doxy didn't have Percival's knack for holding laughter at bay, and it showed as he stood, kissed her forehead, and headed out behind Percy.

The healers bowed, their boxes of herbs and tools held in their hands before them, "Miss Adeline."

She sighed, standing with an effort and groaning. She caught her breath, only to eye the hard surface and wish she were anywhere but where she was. Addy gathered her wits and lay on her stomach.

"Did you have ice, my lady?"

"Don't ask," Adeline begged, turning her face into her hands on the table.

Chapter 9: Meddlesome Meddlers

"Doxy's little sister is amusing." Fedvich stated nonchalantly around a mouthful of buttered herbal bread.

The Seven were back at the castle, enjoying their usual dinner together with the Duchess Insatiable. The hunt lasted until evening, with the final lord arriving to retrieve his prize at five. Most of the perfumed ladies requested a few dances afterward.

Harry sniffed his hands and made a face, "I still smell like roses. Did little Pomm smell like roses?" Not that he hated the scent. The ladies were overcome with love for that perfume this season.

"No." Fedvich leaned over, sniffing Harry's palms as well and shaking his head. "Better wash up before you go see your precious stone."

"Again?" Slayth asked, his brows raised.

"Like it's any different from any other time we've been home." Charn added, "Every night he's free, he's hers."

"Let her be working," Slayth said as if praying. "Remember the last time she wasn't there?"

"Gods." Fedvich groaned, "Never heard the end of her charms he missed out on."

"I'm going to stop talking altogether." Harry claimed, hurt, that his friends complained so much about the love of his life.

"Please do." Many of the men in attendance said in unison.

"Sirs, please." Duchess Virsin chimed in, "It's not like he hasn't listened to you all about your conquests, or wives. Let him have his moment. I think it's cute that he's finally in love."

"Cute?" Harry stared down the table at her, "Cute?"

"Another word for precious. Like a puppy. Like a Pomm," Fedvich added, giving Doxy a long look.

Harry wanted to throttle Fedvich, but upon seeing the come-hither-stare he decided not to step in on that explosion.

Sam Wicker

"I gather most Pomms are of the adorable portion of the lords and ladies." Virsin smiled, looking between Doxy and Fedvich, then studied Harry. "Miss Adeline might be enough to tempt one of you gentlemen."

"No. No, she won't. Not a temptress. Not at all adorable, nor cute. She's mean; a harpy." Doxy cried, fists squeezing open and closed on either side of his forgotten plate. "She doesn't smell like roses but of... horses and sweat." His cheeks heated as he struggled for more insidious claims, "And... and more sweat."

"Well, she won't mind the sweat of a good ride, will she?"

Doxy's mouth hung open, eyes wide on Harry. He began sputtering half-words. His hands flew up, down, created fists, and at last a finger pointed shakily at Harry.

"Harry, fix him." Regus ordered quietly with narrowed eyes.

Harry enjoyed watching Doxy get flustered, it was one highlight of his days. "Now, see here, Doxy. You know I only give rides to the willing." He stood, wiping his mouth with a napkin before tossing it on his plate and strolling around the table to place a hand on Doxy's shoulder. He whispered in the boy's ear, "Besides, I'm sure I have your blessing... considering I have a few chittering furred friends at the ready..."

The sputtering grew worse, Doxy's left eye twitching.

Fedvich's brows drew together, "That's not fixing."

Virsin chimed in with some news: "Miss Adeline is to be my guest for tea the day after next. I'll introduce her to the good boys, so be on your best behavior. All of you."

Harry laughed, patting Doxy on the shoulder, "I'm joking! But she isn't." He waved a hand to the room, bowing grandly before showing himself out.

The parlor Madame ushered him into was all softness of velvet traced in white and black laces. The drapes were thick, as if the darkness of night wasn't dark enough. She sat across from him, the squat round table between them slowly filling with sweets and hot tea as Clover and another whore served them.

Garnet must not be here yet. It wasn't that she had another client. The idea of another man enjoying her whips was enough for him to break through these walls. No, she was his. His alone.

When did he become so naïve?

"Now then, Sir Red," the Madame began, "Let's enjoy some tea together." Her spidery hand waved over the spread between them.

"Do you often host guests while they wait for their lady of choice?" Harry asked leaning forward to pluck a thick white cake topped in cream off the top plate of the decorative three tier treat display. He put the whole tiny thing into his mouth and regretted it. The cake was dry.

"Not all guests, no. But you are a favorite." With that last word her face twitched and twisted, making her thin wrinkles distort around her mouth and bright blue eyes.

Harry waited to laugh until he had washed down the cake. "Is that so?" He leaned back, not daring to try any of the other sweets for fear of choking. "Seems I remember someone screaming that I was a menace to society and one day she was going to cut my balls off."

He watched the Madame sip her tea, daintily. She placed her cup back on the saucer and the pair made it back to the table in front of her. Her age spotted hands folded in her lap over the blue silk of her dress.

His gaze flicked to the painting behind her. A much younger Madame smiled down at him, her beauty defying the aged being before him that she had become. She still had the same sharp eyes that saw through all the bullshit and caught every coin that walked through her doors. "Pity you didn't have a daughter."

"If I did, you wouldn't ever see her, Sir Red."

"Oh?" Harry sneered as he returned to meeting her glare, "Does that mean you have a child of your loins out and about in this world?"

The Madame waved a hand dismissively, "Mistress Garnet is not here."

"Why not?" He completely forgot to tease her more.

"She's taking a much-needed night off." The Madame added with a sweet smile that turned Harry's stomach, "But there are other mistresses ready and willing, Sir Red. They do miss your company."

Why did her suggestion feel like cheating? "Is she well?"

The Madame sighed yet again, "She is well, you needn't worry."

"Let me buy her debt." Harry leaned forward, watching the sharp eyes.

"We've had this discussion, Sir Red, many times. Too many, in fact. Her debt is none of your concern."

He clenched his fists. "Then let me buy another."

Her face lit up, the wrinkles seeming to grow thin, "Of course! Which one shall we discuss?"

"Why is it that I can purchase another Mistress, but not Garnet? Do you have prejudice against her?" Harry's brow twitched as the Madame's countenance darkened. "Or is it that she doesn't want me?"

"She has no debt with me."

There were those words again. Garnet had to be doing this for pleasure, then. Or was there something else? "Does she have debt with someone else causing her to work here?"

"That is for you and her to discuss."

"She won't discuss it with me!" Harry slammed his fist on the table, the porcelain rattling with his anger. He sucked in a breath through his nose, and let it out slowly through his mouth. "Tell me, Madame, how am I to gain her?"

"Sir Red, you are a fine man with more power at your disposal than most in your station because of your... comrades. I'm sure if you stopped thinking with your dick long enough and gave your brain a run you can manage her." The Madame's smile was a wicked thing, "Now leave me before you break something and I have to break your pretty little face."

He chuckled to fight back the rage and pain at being denied again, "Very well, Madame."

Chapter 10: Baby! What Baby?

Year before Survival of Bertran, 25 years ago
"Ricky!"

He pivoted at the nickname, a grin spreading, and he knew he looked a fool. He caught the slim form of his favorite sister, letting her wrap around him. Harry hugged her back, squeezing tightly as she giggled. "Number three seems happy today."

"Number seven is starting that ridiculous numbers game I abhor. Seems he wants to be pinched!"

Harrick laughed, jerking away from the sharp pinch to his back.

"Gods, where did all this muscle come from?" She asked, patting his back, then sliding off him to squeeze his biceps with both hands.

"You've been gone for a year, sis." Harry leaned in, resting his forehead against hers, "You shouldn't have come back."

Tears sprang into her eyes, "I didn't have a choice."

Harry followed the sideways glance. He growled, causing the guards to retreat with raised palms. He met her gaze again, "Rylah, you need to run away."

"Not without you, my sweet brother." She said, cupping his face in her hands with the saddest smile he'd ever seen on her pretty countenance.

"I'm not finished here."

"Harrick, they'll kill you. I'm surprised they haven't already."

"I think I'm feared enough, and father is distracted." He shuddered as his mind fed him images of the last time he'd stumbled upon the man. It was a scene he hoped he wouldn't have to see again. At least not until he killed the tyrant.

"Fear isn't adequate. Not for them. We need to go. We need to run away, please, Ricky." Rylah's hands slipped into his hair, tugging gently at the strands just behind his ears. She used to do that instead of twisting his ears when she caught him being naughty.

He liked the same cookies as Rylah, and often bribed the cook better than she did.

"You didn't see what they did to Yarra because of me. Because of what I did to Semir." He could still hear her sobs if he allowed himself to be in the quiet. He had nightmares filled with the screams of Yarra, his mother, and the other innocents that his family destroyed. "I have to at least make up for that."

"Revenge is not a good look on you." Rylah said quietly, pulling away to sit on the plush pillows at their feet. She eyed the fire burning high in the pit in the middle of the black stone room. The orange flames flickered in her eyes before she turned back to look up at him, "It'll eat you alive."

Harrick crouched beside her, plucking at the loose blue dress sleeve, "Freedom looks good on you. I'll help you get back out. But this time, you need to run far enough away for them not to reach you."

Rylah shook her head, "I need to get out to see him again." She smiled, her hazel eyes lighting up with it as she grabbed his hand and whispered hurriedly, "Ricky, you'll love him. He's funny, and loving. He's given me so much in just the two months I've known him. Even a baby."

Harry snorted, "Two months? Rylah, how do you suppose he's not a plant, and that's how they found y- baby? What baby?"

His eyes shot to her stomach, as did one of his hands. She felt normal there, no more rounded than she had ever been. He yelped when she smacked his hand and met her gaze. Harry rolled his eyes at himself, "Yeah, I know. Babies just don't make you balloon right off..."

Fear gripped his heart. Rylah was in greater danger than ever before. If some of their siblings found out... no, if their father found out. He jerked his palm away from her stomach and looked around to make sure no one was with them.

"Harrick." She said softly, "I understand."

He met her gaze again, "Ry, you really shouldn't have come back."

"I wanted to tell you. And I need your help. I want you to be with me forever. I can't protect you when I'm gone."

He snorted, then sobered when her brow shot up and her jaw set. In her eyes, he was still the toddler sobbing each time someone screamed. What could he do?

Harry excelled at escaping, yet guilt compelled his return each dawn following his nightly releases. He had those he wanted to protect, to keep alive, and he had those he wanted to kill but lacked opportunity. The fact that Semir's death was a mere ripple in the evils of the castle helped him stay alive. The only one who cared about the kill, his father, and Harry figured the old man was just waiting for a prime time to make an example of him.

His father liked a spectacle.

"Remember what I showed you to get you out this last time? That path still stands, and is still protected. Use it to meet your lover, husband... are you married, too?"

Rylah shook her head, "No. Are you sure?" Her face brightened, "His name is Geppi."

"Yes, I use it almost every night. I'll go with you, just to keep an eye on you." Harry repeated the name, memorizing it the best way he knew how.

"I can take care of myself."

Harry admonished with a motion to her belly, "It's not just yourself now, Ry."

"Right."

He sighed; how did he get her back out to safety?

Eight months of planning was useless.

Harry hit his knees, clutching the stone wall that blocked him from falling to his death from the parapet. Below, guards dragged Rylah and her lover into the castle. His body shook all over, his vision narrowed as his lungs didn't want to fill with the cold air. He had been so careful. What had happened?

The baby.

Harrick pushed off the wall, half crawling, half stumbling into a run to fly down the curled staircase of the tower. Rylah couldn't die. Rylah couldn't be sullied. The baby needed to survive.

Sam Wicker

To Harry, that child was hope. Hope for a better future, for a better family, for more love and less hatred. He wanted to show that child beauty and kindness. He wanted to make sure the world survived his father so he could show the child those things.

Rylah hadn't screamed in years.

But he still knew the sound. He knew the echo bouncing off the stone walls over his own echoing footfalls down the west hallway, then into the main one. Another of her screams and he felt the burn of his own tears before they blurred his vision.

Harrick knew the torture chamber that was the throne room well.

He didn't have to push open the double doors. They were wide, letting everyone witness the show. The King had Rylah at his feet, her long red tresses tangled over his fingers and gripped in his large fist. Her belly, huge, lay bare, the green dress torn to shreds and hanging limply from her limbs.

Rylah stared at the men in the middle of the room. The second son's ass bounced as he buried his cock into the man before him. Each thrust caused blood to gush onto the floor from the lover's wound. Geppi's face was pale, except for the blood that covered it when he was pressed into the pool.

With a growl, Harrick ripped his brother off Geppi, pulled his dagger from his thigh, and stabbed the still hard dick through. He twisted the blade, finishing the organ with a yank. Harry kicked the knees out from under his godsforsaken brother and mimicked the hold his father had on Rylah. "She is to be unharmed."

He hoped with all his might and silent prayers that his one loyal servant in this hell was doing his duty. If Rylah was to return, his servant was to contact a friend, and that friend would take Rylah as soon as Harrick got her out of the castle. He couldn't afford to have that plan go awry, too.

"Is it your child, then?" His father's voice droned as if bored with life.

Harry ran through a few scenarios following the three answers he could give. Giving himself time by pricking his brother's neck and making him scream like the coward he was. He had to choose the correct one. He hoped he chose the right answer. "Yes."

The brightness that crossed his father's face made him gag. The jagged teeth, covered in obsidian, gleamed in the light of the several chandeliers and large floor to ceiling windows behind the throne. He glanced at Geppi and nearly gagged again. The dark, tall man who gave his sister so much love didn't move. His breath didn't stir the blood pooling around his nose and open mouth. "That one was her chosen lover, but he's seedless. I made sure of it, so mine would be the seed that would take."

"Why was she out?"

"I allow her holidays with the lover. A happy woman makes a healthy babe, right?" His attempt at humor fell flat in his shaking voice. The lies came easy to him, that wasn't the problem. The problem was the tyrant was still holding his sister hostage, and the baby.

"If you need your women to be sated by another, you should learn more from the Son of Gachent. Send for him."

Send for him? Fedvich? Hope sprang in his chest. Fedvich had joined the enemy. Fedvich could protect her. The Son of Gachent was the better course to take.

Harrick nodded, "Yes, of course, Father." The name slid from his lips but made his stomach flip. He felt greasy, nasty, admitting he came from the repulsive oaf lazing naked on the throne.

"Now take her and fuck her until she screams again. She has the best ones, don't you think?"

Harry stuck the blade in his brother's throat as soon as Rylah was at his side. "He's useless without a dick." He said with a shrug, pressing Rylah to his back as he walked slowly backward.

"That he is, good job."

Chapter 11: Of Leather and Lace

She had freshly polished her boots. The fine footwear was well worn, from her toes all the way up her thick calves, to her knees. The leather of the whip scraped along the scruff of his jaw, stopping at his chin and making him look up, up into the black mask with white lace covering it.

Those green eyes made his heart pound.

"I met someone like you today, sir."

He worked some of the excess saliva out of his mouth, peering into one eye, then the other, "Oh? Maybe I have a brother I don't know about. What was his name?" He caused fingernails to rake against his spine with the idea one of his few remaining siblings could be here.

With each click of her tongue, she tapped the thick leather neck against his chin. The tails brushing his clavicles with each move sent gooseflesh all over him. She hadn't whipped him yet, and the anticipation was palpable. He needed to kill whomever she met.

"Watch yourself, sir."

He closed his eyes, letting her voice sink into his memory, and warm his body. "What was his name, Mistress Garnet?"

She laughed, slapping the tails against his chest. "There are no real names here, you know that. Nice try."

"Was he more to your liking than I am, Mistress? Is that why you mentioned him?" He straightened, taking the chains into his hands to relieve the pressure of the shackles around his wrists.

"Hmm, perhaps," she said thoughtfully, tapping the handle against her palm. "He was rather chivalrous. An attribute difficult to find in lords these days." She stopped tapping, her lace-covered hand drifted toward him. She touched his shoulder.

His breath caught. Her touch was light. Thrilling, but he wanted more. He always wanted more. "I'm considered chivalrous.

And charitable. Kind." Her laugh washed over him and caused him to shiver expectantly.

"Mischievous, needy, and full of lust more like."

She dropped to a crouch in front of him. He looked down at her upturned face; the lips, painted a bright red, beckoned him. "Only for you, Mistress Garnet. I desire you more than life." Something flickered in her eyes at his words, and his heart jumped. "If you would allow it, I can buy your debt. Free you. Protect you."

"Perhaps you are a little chivalrous." She trailed her hand over his shoulder, down his biceps as she spoke. "Once you bought me, Sir Red, what then? You have your way with me for a few months before I bore you and you save to buy another that catches your desire?"

"No." His answer was quick, and he drew back, surprised at himself. "No, Mistress. I would devote myself to you." Harry's entire body ached for her. One little lace-covered touch wasn't satisfactory this night.

"How many stripes does your devotion hold?"

He gazed upon her magnificence as she stood before him once more. She wore too many layers. "All of them. All you can give. I swear this: I am yours and yours alone."

"I almost believe you. Is this how you broke the other mistresses?" Her smile was weak, trembling. As she fanned herself with one hand, she said, "I cannot say as I blame them for giving in to you."

His heart dropped, and he hung by the shackles as he stared up at her. She didn't believe him. Not even a bit. "I know that was solely lust, Mistress." He forced words out of his mouth, trying to formulate more to say to make her heed him. "What I have for you is love."

"Let's beat that charm out of you before I do something I regret."

Her voice changed, disappointment? Or was it something else? Harry twisted, trying to maintain eye contact as she circled behind him. "I would have you regret nothing." He hissed, jerking forward as the first strike was harsher than any she'd ever landed

on him before. "What is your debt? I'll pay it. Prove it all to you."
The slap of leather drowned his words.

He wasn't sure she had heard him. Or if she cared to listen.

"Regus, I need a flight tag." Harry didn't bother knocking before entering Regus' office. If he and Virsin were at it again... Well, it wouldn't be the first time he'd interrupted them. He was sure it wouldn't be the last.

"Lily?" Regus asked with a glance up at his second as he reached into the bottom drawer where he kept the spelled tags for dragon flight.

"Yeah, I've been neglecting her of late." Harry caught the tag, feeling the spell through the tingles it caused on his palm and fingertips. He needed some time to sort his thoughts and plan his next move with Garnet. He still couldn't believe he had confessed to her so readily. Would she even want a dragonkin?

Since King Gervin's rule began off the backs of The Seven, dragons needed permission to shift from someone of the royal court outside of the yearly or bi-yearly flights. It was to aid in reducing fear, and the traumatic symptoms of those who had faced a Tearney dragon during the war. Harry didn't mind it. It made his job of taking care of Lilyanna from afar easier as dragons were not a common sight since the new ruler took the throne.

"You mean she's getting more difficult for Rix to handle?" Regus chuckled with a shake of his head. "How long are you going to be gone this time?"

"Not even a day. Fedvich is fixing me up with some speed to help with that." Harry answered readily while thinking of poor Rix. He wondered if he paid the boy enough to watch over his niece night and day. Tearneys were not known to be easy wards.

"I'm sure you know the disappointment you shall face should you miss Virsin's tea party with Ms. Pomm."

Harry tapped the golden and black lettered tag against his temple. "Never fear, I wouldn't miss making Doxy squirm for the world, sir." He grinned as Regus rolled his eyes. With that he left the Norvasos castle to enter the training grounds again. In the center was a small pack of his clothes and necessities just in case he should need to kill someone, something, or stay more than he anticipated.

Fedvich stood over his pack, a glow about him as his lips moved in silent concentration. It took a lot out of a witchkin for them to use their powers on someone else. Harry began stripping, tucking his discarded clothes into his pack. He pressed the tag against his chest, hissing as it sank into his flesh and etched itself on his skin from chin to navel.

"Good?" He asked Fedvich.

The other redhead's lips twisted, "You know better than most how good I am."

Still a teasing narcissist even as sweat beaded his brow with holding magic. Harry rolled his eyes a little, "I'll remind myself of that once I get back. Think of it as payment for your time and efforts."

Fedvich snorted, "This is worth much more than a nice fuck, Harry." He frowned, "You gonna shift or are we gonna stand here all evening? Not that I mind staring at you naked, never have minded that, but you have somewhere to be."

The familiar thrill of being praised and noticed by Fedvich settled over his skin in goosebumps. Some things never changed. Harry grabbed the back of Fedvich's neck and planted a kiss on those smug lips before stepping back and beginning the change.

He continued to move backward as his body stretched and cracked. It wasn't painful, not for him, because he hadn't spent too long in one form or another. Shifting into his scales was like taking the time for an extra long and rolling stretch right after waking up from a deep slumber. Once his body was the size of the royal carriage, his scales began taking over his skin, clicking and clacking into place. He watched the ruby red plates cover him with a smile. He wasn't as narcissistic as Fedvich, but he knew the color of his scales was downright gorgeous. The only thing marring his beauty was the letters of the tag, and Regus' emblem of shield and sword, letting anyone that saw him in flight know he had permission from Norvasos. He filled the training grounds. He curled around Fedvich with ease and lifted his leathery wings high with a fluttering stretch.

Sam Wicker

Fedvich placed his hands between his raised nostrils, his palms warm even against his scales. Another tingle made his scales shift and clack together as the magic poured over him from his friend. He then turned his head, rubbing his cheek against Fedvich's body.

"Yeah, I know, I'd still want to fuck me too." Fedvich chuckled, running his hands along the ridge of scales over Harry's golden eye. "Bring our little girl back if she's in trouble, Harry. We're settled now. I think she'd be happy here."

Sure. Happy with a bunch of men that her uncle will kill if they look at her for a second. Me on the other hand... Harry grumbled his discontent.

"Right. Perhaps she'd be too in love with the smell of testosterone in the morning. That's the only reason why I stay." Fedvich's grin was weak, sweat still dripping off his brow.

Get some rest. I'll be back tomorrow. With that Harry scooped up his pack in his front paw, and jumped up to let his wings catch the air and pull him up into the sky. Fedvich's speed had him up above the clouds in two flaps. His eyes watered, but the thrill of power added to his own strength made his heart pound and a wide show of sharp teeth to the world to appear.

What would have taken him three hours' time, took him an hour and a half. The way back was going to drag even more now that he'd tasted Fedvich's speed. He was hovering over the town, deciding where to land when he felt the spell fade away. The lack of power felt as draining as being let down from a greatest hope. No wonder witchkin were so stingy with their spells. It could easily become addictive.

He circled again, and settled on the garden right behind the house Lily was in. Dropping into it, he hoped the roses and the overgrown hedge wasn't expensive or sentimental. Nor the bird fountain he swatted into dust with his tail and back leg. Cursing under his breath, he shifted back before he destroyed anything else.

"Uncle Harry!"

He should have thought this through better. The girl was about to pounce on him and he would be naked. He watched his niece bound out of the double doors, a wide grin plastered on her face. His breath caught. She looked more and more like Rylah with each passing year.

A flash of black, and Lilyanna was caught and turned back toward the house.

Thank the gods for Rix. Even if the man was glaring at him through the slit in his mask. Noted.

"Rix! Stop this! Let me go!"

Harry pulled out his pants and put them on, giving Rix a nod once he had them tied in place.

The bodyguard stopped wrestling Lilyanna away. The girl, no, she was a woman now, huffed and bolted for him. Harry held his arms wide and caught her with a grin. He twirled her around, holding her tight.

His heart swelled even as tears burned his eyes at the thought of how he wished Rylah were here to dote on her daughter. He willed his emotions to steady themselves before he set her back on her booted feet. He looked down into her brown eyes, and wiped away her tears. Gods, why was it so difficult to see her? But he didn't want to ever leave her, either. "There's my beauty." Harry murmured as he cupped her face in his hands and leaned down to press his forehead to hers. "I have missed you, Lilyanna."

"You wouldn't have to miss me if you would just take me with you."

The fire in those words ripped through him even as he chuckled at her audacity. If he could get Garnet, marry, build a house, he could protect Lilyanna and give her a steady loving home like she deserved. If. "Maybe our dreams of being a family together will come true sooner than we both think."

Her brows raised toward her curly red hair. She placed her hands on his wrists and canted her head to study his eyes one at a time. "Truly?"

When he nodded, she tackled him to the ground with a giggle.

Chapter 12: Pick of the Litter

"Adeline! We had an agreement." Her mother's palms were on her hips, and those drawn-on brows were high toward her tightly bunned gray hair.

"I can't help you had five sons and the only one that likes to cook is living at the barracks!" Adeline shot back, then squealed, trying to hide behind the book in her hands. Her mother put down the vase of hydrangeas as if she hadn't threatened her daughter with it.

"I have four sons and a daughter. Four. While you may act like a male half the time, you have the desires of a woman and the form of one. You only claim malehood when you don't want to hold up your part of our arrangement." She tapped the toe of her boot against the polished marble floor, "Come."

Adeline groaned, "Do I have to?"

Viscountess Pomm sighed heavily, "My dear, I understand, I truly do. But you're already dressed for it, why waste all that time?"

She hated when her mother used logic against her. "Fine." She eyed her slippered feet on the other side of the chaise. Resting on her back provided the most ease, although her pain lessened since the healers intervened. Closing her book over an old letter from Doxy she sat up, then stood. "The carriage ride is going to be such fun. So comfortable."

"Sarcasm does not suit you."

"Does it suit anyone?" Addy waddled with her mother from the eastern-facing drawing room and down a portrait-filled hallway. A large family meant many sittings for paintings. One every three years.

The last one was two years old. Another year of freedom from primly sitting still with farting brothers for hours. Time enough to come up with an excuse. Perhaps she could join Doxy in the barracks, for he'd missed the last, and had been painted in afterward.

Exiting the hall, they crossed the rounded foyer of white stone and dark wood doors and banisters. Thin windows with thick glass lent the tall entryway sunlight. A small crystal chandelier hung unlit, but made rainbow spots dance through the room as the wind whipped through the door once their footman pulled it open for them.

"That is worse than I thought." Her mother admitted, sliding her gloves on and fitting the lace between each finger with a quick clasp of her hands.

Adeline's pale-yellow skirts pushed against her legs as she followed her mother toward the door. Their butler handed her a pair of gloves and a matching little hat with tiny flowers along the brim. She didn't bother with the hat until safely inside the carriage.

"Here." Her mother reached for her, smoothing her dark blonde hair back down into the twists before putting her hat on, pinned askew.

"Where to today, Mother?" Addy asked, slipping her white gloves on and mimicking her mother's move to make them fit her fingers. The wind whistled through the small openings between the carriage doors and windows.

The carriage jolted forward, and Adeline gritted her teeth. Her rear was as whole as it could be, but the healers said the bone was broken. The bones fused, or something similar. They stated the nerve recovery could require far more time. This jerky carriage ride would not aid in the healing, but could make her adrenaline rise.

Along with her mother's grin.

"Shopping."

Addy whimpered, then whined, "Mother, we shopped last month." When her mother's right brow twitched and her lips tightened, Addy sat up straight and tried again without the tantrum, "We shopped last month, why so quickly?"

"I'm afraid we should marry you off soon, my darling daughter," Viscountess Pomm said with a small smile. "We've received two offers since the hunt. You must have made an impression."

Sam Wicker

The only men she'd talked to were her family, Fedvich, who
was interested in another Pomm, and the duke, who was happily
sated in marriage. "I didn't converse with any single lords,
Mother."

"I assume you conversed with Duke Victory, did you not?"
Her mother asked, eyes steady on her daughter's face.

"I did, yes, for a moment." What did that have to do with
anything?

"You impressed him. There is an invitation to take tea with
the duchess. I suppose she is to introduce you to some of their
single vassals." A hint of uncertainty or worry laced her mother's
words.

"I won the tea through the hunt, but there was nothing said
of... picking from the litter?" She shook her head, trying to clear it
of the racing questions, "Isn't that odd?"

"Strange, yes, but it might be a good thing." Her mother
added, "You leisurely picking will give your father time to get used
to the idea. I don't believe any of your brothers would challenge a
beau trained and hardened by war. Doxy would be your only
worry, but even he fears the other members of The Seven if you
were to choose one of them. I think there are still three who are
single, perhaps four."

As her mother reasoned through the preferred choices for
Addy via the duchess, she let her eyes wander. Outside the
carriage she could see shoppers, workers, and more on the
sidewalks before the bright shops and duller trades buildings.
Narrow alleys led to slightly wider streets with more stores, or
further into the factory district. Within minutes, they would move
back into a shopping district, mainly dedicated to ladies, featuring
only two men's clothing shops and cafes.

As she watched a few children make a game of dodging the
adults while running down the street, Addy knew she would have
to rely on the duchess' judgement on The Seven. Doxy was bound
to clam up and deny that any of them were worthy.

I would devote myself to you.

Last night, those words sent a new thrill trailing up her
back. This morning, they did the same. Foolish. The redheaded
submissive declared that to every mistress, she was certain.
Unless... unless he didn't.

It didn't matter. He was not for her. When she married, she would never see him again. His strength and long hair made him either a performer or... one of The Seven.

They all had long hair.

Adeline wasn't sure what it meant when her face heated, her stomach fluttered, and her hands grew clammy all at once. Was she to fan herself or to make the carriage stop? Did she suddenly come down with a cold? Was that possible?

"Addy?"

How could one catch a cold within a rocking and rolling contraption in this heat?

"Adeline!"

Her mother's voice was sharp, and Addy gaped at her, unsure what was said and what wasn't.

"Adeline, are you well? You look positively undone."

Her mother pressed a palm to her cheek. The butterflies in her belly stilled with the touch. Her clammy hands stopped trembling as she squeezed her fingertips against her palms.

I desire you more than life.

Gods fucking, what was wrong with her? "I am not entirely sure, Mother. I am overcome with some affliction..."

"Perhaps it is nervousness." Her mother took her hands, "Never fear, my dear. You are well, and there is no choice you cannot handle."

Choice. Right. "What was the other inquiry?"

"What? Oh! A man wanted an audience with Doxy, but I assumed they meant you. What man would write for a mother's approval for one of her sons?" Her mother smiled with a gentle giggle. "Nevertheless, such a mistake makes a terrible impression."

Doxy was popular.

What I have for you is love.

Her chest hurt more than it had last night when he spoke so fervently. Did this mean his words were true? Or was her silly heart far too hopeful? Foolish?

"You are still quite pale. Let's try your dress for the tea with the duchess, then we will go back home. Perhaps next week we shop. Yes?"

Sam Wicker

Adeline nodded, trying to shove last night's activities into the recesses of her mind. They belonged there during the daylight. They should remain in the shadows during the night.

Chapter 13: A Chase of the Heart

"Harrick Tearney! Sit!" Regus bellowed, pointing to the corner of the training grounds where the benches crouched haphazardly.

He tossed his practice sword in with the shattered remnants of the wooden dummy. It was the third one he'd made splinters out of this day. Stalking to the corner, he threw himself down on a bench and stared up at the cloud-covered sky.

Not a single drop of rain, but the sun hid.

Harry knew he was acting like a petulant child. Taking all his anger and despair out on whoever came near him was not his normal release. Garnet was his liberation. But now, she was the reason for the shards in his chest. He'd had a broken heart before, but he did not remember it being this painful. Nor did he recall being this angry.

He deserved a good beating, yet none present could best him to improve his mood. Regus would kill him. While there were moments between the anger where death seemed like the answer, Harry couldn't allow it. He still believed Garnet would come around. He had to prove himself to her.

"Harry?"

"No, stay away." He sat up, eyes wild when they found the duchess, "I am not in the mood, and I fear I shall harm you."

Virsin just kept striding toward him.

Harry shook his head, holding his hands out. "Please..."

Pain slashed over his cheek, and his vision swung from the beautiful wife of his duke to the benches. The coppery taste of blood filled his mouth, and he spat. Running his tongue around, he found the cut inside his lip.

"Do you need another?"

Harry licked his lips, returned his gaze to the little terror before him, "Maybe." He pointed to his other cheek, not hiding the grin.

How did married women clear his head with one sound slap? Was a wedding bond such magic? Perhaps it was the threat of their husbands rearing behind them, too.

"I will wait until you say something ridiculous. I know you will." Virsin shook her hand, "I am not sure that hurts you more than it pains me."

Harry chuckled, taking her hand in his, turning it and kissing her palm. "You are a dearly beloved woman in my life." He watched Virsin's brows rise, so he added, "Never fear. Friendship is our bond, my little slappy sweet."

"Ooof, that was rough."

"Too much? Worse than Duchess Insatiable?"

"Yes, I shall have to say yes." Virsin nodded, joining him on the bench. "Did the owner of the gem lady turn you down again?"

Harry sighed, rubbing his temples as he spat blood out again, "I didn't talk to her. I went straight to Garnet."

"Oh."

He could feel Virsin's gaze, but refused to meet it. He didn't like the idea of seeing pity there. "She thought I was joking. After her like I'm after other mistresses."

"Were you after other mistresses? No, are you after others?" Virsin asked.

"No. I was. Not am. I want her. Just her." His heart lurched, and he growled, "Does your chest hurt?"

"Oh, Harry." Virsin's hand was on his cheek, "I hurt when Reg was ignoring me, yes. You're definitely in love."

His sigh didn't relieve any of the pressure in his chest, "I am." He finally looked in her dark eyes, "Please don't tell anyone. I beg you."

She snorted, "I hate to break this to you, but they all know." Virsin motioned to Tim bandaging up Slayth, and then to the wood shards. "You don't hide your emotions well."

Harry followed her hand, grimacing as he realized she was speaking the truth. "No, I don't. I should work on that."

Virsin giggled, patting his cheek. "Good luck, but I doubt you will make any straightforward path toward hiding such things."

"Thank you for the vote of confidence, Duchess. I appreciate it." Harry sighed again, throwing himself back on the bench. "Now leave me, I deserve this break from your husband's torture training."

"Mistress Garnet is not here."

Harry felt his face twitch. He had an impression she would order them to deny him. "What is her debt? What do I do to gain her?" He met the hardened gaze of the Madame. Age created crow's feet at her eyes, and lines around her mouth, and a little loose skin, but she was still gorgeous. Or she would be if he weren't in love with another.

To him, at this moment, she looked like a crone barring him from freeing someone in her dungeon.

"Boy, she is not for you."

"I have money. Let me get her out of this lifestyle." Harrick drew himself up to his full height, towering over the Madame.

"She wants to be here." The hag spat, wagging a finger in his face, "Just like you, she finds pleasure in these activities!"

Something clicked together, piece by piece: nice boots, a new dress each night, and her own private room. The last tea time with the madame. "She's... is she a lady?"

The crone grinned, "Took you long enough."

"Please... let me talk to her." Harry looked from one blue eye of the Madame to the other, watching for any indication. Any sign that she would give in to him.

"I told you, she's not here."

Harry cursed under his breath, about to depart when a door down the hall opened. Her door. He froze, seeing her lace-covered hand, hearing her laugh, and then she was in the hall. He met her gaze.

"Fuck."

She fled from him before Harry got anything further from her. He shoved past the crone, shaking off her sharp talons as she grabbed for him. In his haste, he scraped his shoulders on the narrow walls, bouncing off them until he rounded the corner and entered the other hallway.

"Sawyer!"

Sam Wicker

Her screaming another man's name made his blood boil. She was already at the end of this hall. He grinned, a quick little rabbit his Garnet was. Then his elation faded as Sawyer's bulk filled his path. Literally. His shoulders brushed each side of the wood panels.

Not able to stop, and not willing to, Harry rammed into the man, hoping to bowl him over.

Instead, he flew back, landing on his ass and staring up at the shining bald head and grin of one Sawyer, protector of whores, Grey.

"Sawyer, sir, while I normally commend your efforts, and often join in on them, I cannot allow you to stop me."

"I did. Right then." Sawyer pointed out, chin jutting as his toothy smile took over his pale face.

Harry grunted as he stood, peering over Sawyer's shoulder. Not a skirt or fine boot in sight. "I cannot argue that." He admitted, then bolted back the way he came. There was more than one way to get out of this place.

Sawyer's heavy footfalls shook the boards he ran on. Big bastard. Harry understood fully the damage he could inflict. He passed the crone, who was screaming obscenities and other things at him. He was sure there were a few words in there he didn't know. Harry made a mental note to ask about them later.

The door flew off its hinges with a squeal and crashed to the cobblestones as he jumped through it. His boots skidded on the stones, damp with a misty rain. Pain shot through his shoulder as he hit the crumbling brick wall, but he used it to turn and launch himself down the narrow street. With any luck, he'd meet her on the road he hoped she took. If she were a lady, it was the quickest route back to her part of town.

"You'll pay for this door!"

"Put it on my tab!" Harry bellowed, not bothering to slow or turn around.

His feet pounded, propelling him forward as if Reg was wielding a sword after him with murder in his eyes. He skidded and slid into an alley, turning sideways to slide down the path as quickly as possible, before reaching the other road it intersected. He glanced back, and then ahead.

There, not a block ahead, skirts were high over familiar boots, and the clack of the wooden heels was music to his ears. He had sight of her again. This time, he wasn't about to lose her.

His lungs were burning, but his muscles felt right at home as his stride elongated into a ground-eating gait. The distance closed between them once she swiveled mid-step. There was a shocked little cry, and she turned back around to double her speed.

"What was that, my mistress?" He asked, knowing she couldn't possibly hear him. Whatever that sound was, it made his heart jump. She was very fast. Too fast. He quickly lost whatever ground he'd gained.

The road widened, and he cursed, knowing he had little time to catch her. He doubled his efforts, trying in vain to close the gap. Was she part horse? What was with her speed? Witchkin?

The gates ahead that separated the cheap side from the newly renovated middle class were still closed. He grinned. She had nowhere to go.

Until the gate opened. A copper stepped through. And she bolted through with the cop tapping a thick bar in his palm.

Noted.

Harry slowed, coming to a stop with plenty of room to spare between him and the warden. He held his hands up, his mind going through half a dozen scenarios, none of which ended as he hoped. She was halfway through the row of houses that lined the street. The soft glow of dawn warmed the horizon in front of her.

"Your business with the lady is finished, sir." The cop drawled, still tapping the stick.

Harry blew out a laden breath, then leaned down on his knees. "For now, I must agree."

Chapter 14: Oh, the Pain, the Agony

Oh gods. Oh gods. Oh gods. Adeline sprawled over the dew wet grass of the small garden outside her rooms. She didn't have any lungs left. And she swore her garb had picked up ten pounds of weight somewhere.

Dawn was hovering, threatening to reveal her secret.

Did the man have long limbs, or what? Addy whimpered, rolling to her stomach to cool her face on the grass. Her muscles twanged and cried out in protest. Her calves shot pain up and down her legs. Now she had something to distract her from the ache in her backside.

She needed further training if she continued this pattern, if he pursued her each evening. Better yet, stable a horse at the Madame's. Yes, that was a better plan. He was certainly unable to outpace a horse. Right? She still found it difficult to process that she had outran him.

With a groan, she began her crawl to her window. She thanked the gods Doxy had moved out and allowed her rooms on the ground floor. Otherwise, her secret be damned, there was no way she could climb up to her former balcony in the state she was in.

Addy pulled herself up the wall, pushed open the unlocked pane, and eyed the ledge. She had to do it. When had this window gotten so high? Mentally preparing herself by counting down from ten, she added another five, and another six, before she threw herself over the sill. And hung there, half in and half out of her home and the blessed cover of her room.

"Miss!"

That was not the worst voice she could hear at the moment. Addy lifted her head with effort, and smiled wanly at her maid, "Morning, Tillie."

"You weren't at that... that place, were you?"

"Where else would I go?!" Addy snapped, then pressed her fingertips to her eyelids. It wasn't Tillie's fault a madman ran her all the way home. "Help me, please?"

Tillie was not the most adept woman with her strength. That was made crystal clear with how her feet flew up over her head before she landed on her back, staring up at her white ceiling with little blue scrolling vines painted lightly over it. Once Addy regained air in her lungs, she thanked her maid.

"You are to be ready in half an hour!" Tillie cried, hands fluttering about in front of her apron as she leaned over her mistress.

"I'm sick. Plague."

"That won't work, miss! It's your mother! and the duchess' tea."

Today? No, Tillie had her days mixed up. Surely. It was no use trying to figure out what day it was, Addy had to rely on Tillie's schedule. She sighed, "Half an hour?"

"Yes, miss."

She wondered if the duchess minded her guests walking like an old maid.

The half hour ended up being an hour. The urgency was her mother demanding a quick lesson in etiquette, making it fresh in her wayward daughter's mind. Breakfast wasn't a meal that day. Neither was lunch. They provided snacks in the carriage. Addy was supposed to eat daintily, if at all, once she arrived at the duchy.

Right.

Her abdomen howled once the wheels stopped crunching over the white stones of the drive. This was going to be interesting. Adeline kept begging her stomach to cease, it was good for a lady to starve herself now and then. It added character and more chances of a well-timed swoon. Doxy bounded down the wide steps, a grin on his face. He opened the carriage door and held both hands out.

Adeline hissed, "I'm not to be caught like a child."

"Oh, right?" Doxy's face fell, but he didn't move.

Sam Wicker

Addy waited for a breath, then two. With a roll of her eyes, she placed both her palms in her brother's and hoped for the best. It worked, in a way. Until he dropped her hands and grabbed her up in a spin. Since when had he gotten this strong?

She gave in, closing her arms around Doxy's neck tightly, letting him have his moment as a big brother. It was unlikely for her to argue with a single sibling while staying calm. Often, she just gave up and gave in, for there was nothing else for her to do with them. Percival was the only one she could slightly manage.

Doxy, he was nigh impossible.

"You are not to meet the eye of any of them, understand? Keep your eyes on the duchess, smile at her, and keep your answers short and clipped. Don't show them a single iota of attention." Doxy commanded in low whispers as he set her back on her feet.

"Them?" She tamped down on the rise of irritation at being told what to do.

"Men. Virsin has hand-picked a few she thinks are... well... worthy. None of them are. Not a single one. Do you understand?"

His fingers were tight on her upper arm as they took the steps and entered the duke's castle. Her legs screamed their displeasure, growing tighter with each step. She bit the inside of her cheek to keep from yelling at her brother to slow down or to carry her if he was to maintain his lengthy gait.

"Especially any of The Seven. They're whores and not at all intelligent. Vicious, nasty fellows." Doxy continued, guiding her down the hallway to the right of the foyer.

She didn't get to pause to view the splendor.

"Duchess is going to befriend you. As she should, you two should get along grandly. Be clear in denying any of the men she shows you. Tell her you are to enter the priesthood if you must."

"If I'm to be her friend, how shall I keep up the ruse of holiness?" Addy planted her heels, jerking her arm out of Doxy's grasp. She stood still, willing the tightness in her legs to loosen in her newfound rest.

"We will figure it out if it comes to that." Doxy stared at her, "You're pale. Don't worry, Virsin is a good woman. Mostly." The last was added with a pink tinge cresting Doxy's cheeks.

Did Doxy really have to watch the duke and duchess' activities? Good for him. He might discover a thing or two and Fedvich wouldn't have to be too obvious in his infatuation. That thought was laughable.

She held up a finger when he reached for her again, "You cannot walk like a madman. I'm a lady, remember?"

Her brother snorted.

Addy glared at him, tilting her chin up and crossing her arms, "Really?"

"Of course, Miss Pomm," Doxy drawled, taking her hand and changing his pace to match hers.

"Anything else I should know?" This was better. Wasn't it? Her legs didn't care for any movement. Where was this damnable tea table? On the other side of the castle?

"Never wander. Don't be alone with anyone but me, the duke, or the duchess."

"Will the rest eat me or something?"

"Yes."

Adeline giggled, then laughed so hard her legs protested in cramps. Her joy ended in multiple curses, and her bending in half to stretch the muscles out. Was she truly this out of shape? If one brief run did this to her, she could only imagine if she hadn't had a sense of direction last night.

"Addy, what's wrong? Are you having great pain because of your time? Have you caught a stomach affliction?" Doxy ran a gentle palm slowly up and down her back, his other hand within hers to help her balance.

"No, nothing like that. I just..." Sprinted a few miles to keep out of the grips of a redheaded sex god that makes me wet in more ways than one? No, that wouldn't be good to say. "Rode. Rode too hard."

"Oh, I'm glad you are riding still, but do be careful." Doxy crooned, continuing to rub her back. "Shall I carry you? We're almost there, then you can sit and rest."

"No, that isn't nec-" Addy yelped as Doxy scooped her up, "What are you doing?! Down! Put me down this instant!"

Sam Wicker

"No, you're hurting. I cannot have that." Doxy's face reddened all over as he carried her down the hall. "No one is here to see us."

Adeline covered her face with her hands, "But we are in the duchy!"

"I live here. All is well." Doxy reminded her with a grunt as he shifted an arm under her. "Have you gained weight?"

"That is not something you should ask a lady nor comment on. No, I have not!" Addy glared at her brother's profile. Had she? He was stronger than he had been before he joined The Seven, too. Oh dear, perhaps she should run home every night.

Chapter 15: Let's Talk About Boys, Baby

"Oh my, Doxy Pomm, put her down this instant!"

Adeline wanted to crawl back out of the duchy in shame. At least her brother listened to the duchess. A sharp ache radiated from her heels to her hips once she gained her feet on the smooth shining marble floors. If she ever saw Sir Red again she was going to make him run in place for miles until he felt as she did at this moment.

"Virsin, do take care of her. She's in much pain from riding." Doxy's voice changed from his stern orders to a whining plead.

The change made her stare at her own brother. Had he grown two personalities? Adeline turned to look at the duchess. The woman had her fists planted on her shapely hips, and her chin jutted. Suddenly, Adeline was reminded of their grandmother right before the old woman found a switch.

"Come Adeline, let's get you settled and away from your overprotective brother, shall we?" The Duchess smiled kindly at her, then shot another glare at her brother.

She liked the woman already. Doxy cowered beside her like a scorned puppy and she couldn't help the grin it caused. "Yes, Duchess." The time it took her to get to her chair across from the Duchess was too long. She sat, doing her best to ignore how her muscles screamed at the pressure of her weight being both alleviated and fully placed on her buttocks and thighs. "Thank you for inviting me." She smoothed her skirts. Had the run elongated her legs? Her skirt didn't cover the base of her boots anymore. Why was her chair so soft?

Doxy poured the tea for them.

Doxy poured the tea perfectly. Had she entered a dream? Why would her dream world have Doxy knowing how to serve them?

Sam Wicker

"Well done, it seems you have been paying attention to your lessons." Duchess Virsin smiled up at her brother. "Now, you may go. Tell Regus to give me the list sooner rather than surprising us both with the first visit, hm?"

"Of course." Doxy bowed before he left.

"Are you teaching him how to serve tea? Or did you, I mean." Adeline asked, pinching her skirt between her thumbs and forefingers under the table to keep from fidgeting.

"I am. He's rather good at it. It surprised me when he asked, as you know, most men don't care about the intricacies of serving." Virsin spoke as she fixed her tea with two cubes of sugar. "He didn't ask to learn things when he was younger?"

"Not serving. Swordplay, yes, but nothing like that." Adeline admitted, still in awe and wondering why the change in Doxy's training. "Is he going to get kicked out and thinks he has to be a butler?"

Virsin nearly snorted her tea out of her nose.

"Oh, I'm sorry!" Adeline leaned forward to take up Virsin's napkin off her plate and unfold it for her to use.

"Nothing like that." Virsin giggled, wiping her nose. "Forgive me that was quite unladylike. Being in a house full of men I admit to letting my gracefulness go."

"Oh please, I may not have as many men as you do, but I grew up with four brothers and a father that would rather dote on me than do his duties. I understand." Adeline smiled as the duchess did.

"May I call you Addy, like he does?"

"Of course." Adeline beamed.

"Then call me Virsin." She said before getting distracted by the door opening. Her smile and countenance doubled in brightness as Regus strode in. The duchess lifted her face, and he planted a quick kiss on her lips before straightening.

"I have the order of victims for you ladies to do with as you please. Fedvich is first, as you requested." He held out a small sheet of paper with a twist to his lips.

Virsin took it and read the names quickly before folding the paper and placing it in her lap, "Harry is last and Fedvich is first? I'm not sure that helps Doxy relax at all."

Regus lifted a broad shoulder. "So be it. He needs to learn to calm down and not be so jumpy all the time."

"He is rather dramatic, but that's what makes him adorable. Don't you think so, of your brother, Addy?"

Adeline giggled, "Doxy is cutest when he's flustered."

"Ladies, I leave you to it. Make sure they are still able to clean their gear once you are done with them, hm?"

"I make no promises, Reg." Virsin watched her husband bow, and didn't speak again until the door closed behind him.

"I like you already, Addy. Are you ready to torture some men? I daresay they are the most handsome of the lot, and are a range of personalities to keep you entertained." Virsin turned her attention back to her guest.

"I feel the same." She swallowed, thinking on it for a moment. "What better way to get to know you than to tease them with you?"

"Ah, perfect!" Virsin bounced in her chair. "This first one is going to be the best. He's such a flirt!"

Adeline didn't remember that of Fedvich. She wondered if his forehead was back to normal yet. She didn't have to wait long as he entered and strode toward them. The smirk on his face and the way his eyes stayed on her made Adeline think of a prowling cat.

"Well, hello, little Pomm. We meet again."

"Oh, that's right! You two have met before!" Virsin laughed and motioned for Fedvich to sit down with them. "Our other Pomm steeped this tea to perfection, Fedvich, won't you have some?"

The way Virsin spoke of Doxy with Fedvich let Adeline know she wasn't the only one who knew of Fedvich's adoration for her older brother. It also solidified her guess that it was indeed Doxy he was after. "Is that why I didn't get flirted with like everyone else does?"

Fedvich coughed as he set his tea cup down, "I treated you the same as everyone else, dearest."

"Hm. It's not as impressive as I would think considering your reputation."

Sam Wicker

It was Virsin's turn to laugh again. She hid her mouth behind her napkin and sat back to watch the show.

The redhead leaned on his elbow toward Adeline, propping his chin on his palm. "Should I make you swoon now? I daresay, carrying you all that way after you..." His bronzed gaze flicked to Virsin then back again, "Strength doesn't make your toes curl, darling?"

"After I made you swoon, sir? You know I have four brothers. Strength is like farts, I've had enough of those shows."

"Wait, Fedvich fainted? How did you manage that?!" Virsin leaned forward as well.

"Dearest duchess, that is between me and this lady for we never speak of what happens in the woods." Fedvich countered, his eyes narrowing slightly at Adeline as if relaying a threat. "Adeline, would you like some ice in your tea? You haven't been drinking it yet."

"How kind of you, but I'm enjoying my tea as is. Just as you are, for it's the closest you'll come from drinking of Doxy if you keep this up."

"She's moving in with us." Virsin claimed suddenly.

Fedvich laughed as he leaned back. "Agreed. I do believe she will keep all of us entertained. Now we just have to fit her in with one of our boys so she can."

"Not you?"

Fedvich and Adeline snorted together at Virsin's outrageous suggestion.

"Hardly my type, plus he's in love with my brother. That's too odd."

Virsin nodded, "Agreed. Fedvich, go back and study her choices to help her."

"Yes, madam Duchess." Fedvich chuckled, taking Adeline's hand and kissing the back of it. "Believe me, if I wanted you, you couldn't deny me."

Adeline rolled her eyes. "Save it for Doxy."

Chapter 16: What the Duchess Wills, all the Men Do

"Why are you limping?"

"I'm not. Cannot be. Both feet hurt."

Harry stared right back at Fedvich, narrowing his gaze to match, and also mimicked the long, drawn-out sigh.

"I'm refusing to ask."

"Good. I refuse to tell a damn thing." Harry plopped down and stretched his legs out. He'd worn the wrong boots last night. Never wear brand new boots and run two miles, that was his new rule for life.

"Does she have a new kink for whipping feet or something?"

That would be interesting. Painful yet... no, not a good idea. "Thought you weren't going to ask?"

"I'm not."

"You did."

"Did not!"

"What was that then? 'Does she have a new kink?' How is that *not* you asking what happened when you said you weren't going to? You've been hanging around Virsin too much."

"Gods I hate walking into a room where they've already set up camp." Slayth grumbled, striding into the dining room and taking his usual seat at the large table.

Charn grunted in answer.

"They slapping each other yet?" Bertran asked, using a small pointed twig to dig something out of his teeth as he sat down at the end of the table.

Harry ignored them, but kept his eyes on a few newcomers that were not usually permitted in the dining room with The Seven. Each of them was handsome, had property, not a poor selection for the Pomm lady. If he were to conquer her, and the rest of the Pomms, he was going to have to be extra charming.

Regus walked in when the men were about to enter a heated conversation on whether they should automatically ask Miss Pomm on a date to help impress their duchess or not. In one hand, the duke straightened his collar, in the other was a slip of paper.

He hoped he was going first as the most beloved of the group.

"Bertran, Slayth, you are to keep these men in line. Each one is to have half an hour, unless Virsin sends word otherwise. "Youngest first, but Harry, you are to be last as a favor to Doxy."

"What? Why?" Harry sat up.

Fedvich snorted, "You really have to ask, whipping boy?" He paused, "I've already been, and she's a delight. Far too good for you, my best student. She is not one to be impressed with brawn and tongues."

Harry growled, and those not of The Seven backed away in shuffling steps. "I am the best man here to show a lady a good time."

Charn piped up, "She's a lady, a true one, not one who partakes of nightly activities. You are the least worthy."

"Agreed!" Doxy cried.

Harry whipped his head around, seeing the boy cowering in the doorway. He noted how this was playing out. Here, he thought Doxy liked him, but no. Not well enough to be with the littlest Pomm, apparently. He needed to discuss trapping squirrels with the eldest Pomm as soon as possible.

"Fine. When the rest of you fail miserably, I shall come along and make her day shine in glory." Harry dismissed them all with a flick of his thick ponytail.

The individuals listened to their fearless leader for their tea party entry order. Harry had to admit, Virsin was smart, but he wondered if the first meeting between the ladies was the best time to try her hand at blind dates. Or perhaps he had misheard, and Virsin knew Miss Pomm well enough to pull this stunt. He doubted it. In the year Virsin claimed the duchess title, she hadn't had a single lady nor crone over, not even her family.

Crossing his legs at the ankles after putting them up on the table, he settled back in his chair and closed his eyes. It was going to be a long day. He'd already had a long night.

Fedvich left first, and Harry groused. If Fedvich was first, none of them had a chance.

He didn't fall asleep until he did.

He shot up, hand going to his hip as he heard his name sharp in Regus' voice. He grasped air, then looked down to realize he was again in his dreaded dress uniform. Right, the tea party with the Pomm girl.

"It's your turn."

"Finally." Harry said and stretched. He straightened his clothing as he strode from the room. "Wish me luck?"

"Have you ever needed it?" Regus called out after him.

Harry chuckled, and he made sure his hair was smooth and that no tips caught on his dress jacket. "No, not at all." In a few strides down the wide hall, he entered the drawing room reserved for entertaining guests. Plush furniture, white lace draped over every surface, large floor to ceiling windows to showcase the gray skies. One glorious duchess sat primly across from her delicate guest.

He bowed upon reaching the table.

"Adeline, this is Harrick Tearney, a viscount, and my husband's indispensable second. Harry, this is Miss Adeline Pomm."

Why did those boots look familiar? He asked himself as he chanced to see them under her skirt. He straightened, his eyes trailing over the lady as he smiled. Green eyes. Full red lips. His breath caught.

Silence filled the room as Adeline's mouth dropped to an 'o'. Harry's thoughts whirled. His Garnet. Her round, pretty features resembled what he imagined beneath her mask. He could reach out and touch her.

"Oh, oh, I just remembered... er... Mother... Mother said I mustn't stay long. Forgive me, Duchess!" The porcelain clanked as Adeline rose quickly and bumped the table hard with her hip. "So sorry!"

Sam Wicker

What? What happened? Harry blinked, no longer seeing his beloved sitting at his duchess' table. Gone.

"Why, Harry, whatever did you do to the girl!?" Virsin cried, standing quickly herself and gripping Harry's elbow.

"I..." He couldn't breathe.

"Harry?" Virsin asked. She cried for help when Harry hit his knees before her.

"No. No. I have to..." He stood, his feet not willing to work, for three stumbling steps. He ran through the door, bowling over Doxy and Fedvich in his rush. His legs tangled with the other two, and he cursed, pushing off of them, and half crawling, half standing to gain his feet. "Where did she go?"

"Who?!" Fedvich asked, then cursed as he rose to his hands and knees before holding his groin.

"Garnet!"

"He's gone mad." Doxy lay flat on his back still, panting.

Harry whirled, looking one way down the hall, then the next. "Where? damn you both!"

"Toward the door, where else?!" Fedvich bellowed back, his face purpling.

His legs couldn't launch him fast enough, he stumbled, gaining his feet after two steps to run. This seemed all too similar all too soon. This time, he wouldn't lose her. He was on familiar territory. Not that being in his home had helped him much before.

Chapter 17: It's Never Too Late to Plan a Bloodbath

Year before Survival of Bertran, 25 and a half years ago
"I'm not letting you out of my sight." Harry murmured, taking his sister's hand and tugging her up into his arms.

"Ricky, please. I'm tired." Rylah pushed him away and slumped onto the bed she'd been sitting on the edge of. Her enormous belly caused her to lounge back on the multitude of pillows against the headboard.

"I must meet Fedvich. He's our only hope." Harry's heart couldn't take much more of this. It was one thing to protect a few siblings, innocent strangers, a handful of servants that deserved better masters, and quite another to protect an unborn child. "Please, if he can guide you to safety now..."

"A half-assed plan will not save my child, Harrick." Rylah's red eyes glared up at him as she placed her hands over her stomach. "I cannot plan like you can. What will I do there? Suck him off?"

Harry blinked a few times, "Well, I mean... if you think it'll help convince him..." He grinned when she kicked his shins with the little might she could muster. At least she still had moments where she was herself. Most of the time, Rylah sobbed between being force-fed by Harry himself. "Rylah, I can't leave you here alone."

"We have two guards outside we can trust, and your servants. I'll be fine." Rylah sighed, pushing herself further up onto the bed and turning to her left side. "I'm tired... really tired, Ricky."

His heart broke for the millionth time in the nineteen hours since Geppi's death. It was because Rylah was broken. There was even a moment when she held one of his knives in her hands and began to cut her wrist. Harry had moved all his weapons to makeshift caches on his ceiling.

He'd forgotten how many weapons he'd collected. So many that he had to use linens to make his slings. He'd have someone plug the holes in the ceiling where he'd rammed hooks home once Rylah was safe and his blades could be back within reach for him.

Could Fedvich come here? No, that was out of the question. But he couldn't leave Rylah either. "I can carry y-"

"No."

"Ry, pl-"

"Say please one more time and I'll rip your sack off."

Harry sighed, running a hand over his face as he glanced around his room. Did he dare give her a weapon to protect herself? What if she had another moment of needing to join Geppi? His eyes caught on a corner of wood, and he grinned.

Scaling the walls after growing his claws out, he grabbed the crossbow and the quiver of bolts next to it. With some difficulty, cussing, and dumping the bolts onto the floor below him, Harry came back down. After gathering the bolts back into the quiver, he placed them by her bed, and the crossbow beside her. "Just in case."

"You assume I know how to use this."

"You'll figure it out. Pointy end goes toward the enemy, and the trigger makes the pointy end go in the enemy."

Rylah rolled her eyes, but let him kiss her temple.

Fedvich isn't far from the castle, Harry had to remind himself. He could be back in a flash. He stood and opened the door. After he checked his weapons on his person — at least Rylah hadn't tried for them — he shut the door behind him. His strict instructions to the guards had them both pale, but super alert. That was how he liked them.

Bolting through the castle, he made quick work of the halls, and the foyer out onto the courtyard. He paused, glancing up at the pikes because the number was off. A new one held a half-eaten, once-familiar face. He swallowed the bile, whispering a prayer that Rylah would never see her lover hanging there. When the guard posted below them cleared his throat, Harry raised a brow at him. He smirked, staring down the disdain like he was readying to eat the man like a roasted duck. Of course, the guard looked away first.

He got on his horse and made quick work of the narrow streets. Houses and shacks leaned right up against the castle walls. The city looked horrible. Her streets were uneven, muddy or with more broken stones than solid. The houses were missing basics such as a roof over a corner room, or windows, or even a door. Others were all charred and ash. Gilded gold and silver pillars or frames mocked the surrounding destruction, boasting of a time that once was amid ruins of grand mansions. In the center of the roads, the tyrant's statues stood out, their perfection stark contrasts to their surroundings.

Few held the favor of the king, and their houses were monsters lording over the wreckage of those who had lost respect. The barracks overflowed, usually the only means of survival for most. Only taverns and houses of questionable transactions sported life otherwise. The rest housed skinny children, naked women and men, and the desiccated remains of those who finally gave up.

No matter how much food he sent out, clothing he delivered, or families he hid in wagons, the tyrant found ways to ruin them all.

Harrick slid off his horse at the inn of whitewashed stones and red shutters carved to fit the misshapen windows. The back was against the east wall, but far enough away from the main road leading into the castle that it was often overlooked. It helped that the madam of the inn was a distant cousin on his great-grandfather's side. He took the short steps in one stride, ducking under the low-hanging porch and then through the door.

He scanned the dining room, finding the familiar red easily enough. Harry paused, observing his friend watching a couple sitting across from him at his table. Of course, Fedvich found a way to be entertained while he waited. Never a wasted moment. There was nothing attractive about the skin-and-bones ladies, though.

"Fedvich." When the redhead turned and grinned at him, he jerked his head toward the stairs. He held his hand out for the innkeeper to toss him a set of keys. They climbed the rickety stairs together to the third floor and entered their usual room.

"Harry, I must say, Serland is looking worse and worse." Fedvich said as he closed the door behind them. "If you wo-"

Harry cupped Fedvich's cheek and pressed his thumb to the plump bottom lip, "I know, but I have a more pressing personal matter at the moment."

Fedvich tilted his head, a quick look of lust flashing in his eyes before he noted Harry's countenance. He sighed, then sucked on the tip of the thumb in his mouth before asking, "Why do I get the feeling that I'm not partaking in what one of my favorite students offers tonight?"

His lips twisted before he said, "One of? I am your favorite. And best." He pressed his forehead against Fedvich's, closing his eyes as he dwelled in the security of being in the presence of someone he trusted with his life. "I need you to take Rylah as far from here as you can manage."

Fedvich snorted, "I'd rather pull a rainbow from the heavens for you to wipe your ass with."

"She's... she's not as she once was."

"She'd better not be if she's to be protected by me. I have a scar!" Fedvich loosened the wrap holding his pants tight against his body and pulled both out to point at the tiny line on his hip, dangerously close to his groin. "All because I taught you."

"No, it was because you are a whore, and flirted with her, but that's beside the point." Harry felt lighter, almost as if he could truly smile, but it didn't come. "She's pregnant."

Fedvich froze while straightening his clothes. He then pulled back after his brows drew together, "Is it...?"

"No. She ran away once and fell in love. Father killed him, of course, after dragging her back. I had to tell the tyrant the babe was mine so he wouldn't kill her." Harry said as he turned away and stalked toward the dresser with the drinks on top. He poured himself a glass, took it down in one burning swallow, and poured another. "She tried to kill herself."

There was silence while Harry stared at the amber liquid in the green glass. He wondered whether Fedvich would leave. Harry wondered if there was hope here after all, or if he was delusional.

"Harrick, she will be fine. Once the baby comes, she'll have something she can live for again." Fedvich's voice was soft, as were his hands curling around Harry's waist, and his lips against the side of Harry's neck. "I have news."

Careful of Fedvich's nearness, Harry drank the next glass slower, but still in one go. "What news is that?"

"Have you heard the tale of the Vicious?"

Harry raised a brow, turning to give Fedvich the incredulous look properly, "Everyone has heard of that man. He's the only name that makes father pause in his rutting of corpses and his own daughters."

"I'm with him."

He was glad he'd swallowed the drink. Otherwise, it would have been wasted on the wall, or on Fedvich's face. "As in fucking him or teaching him to fuck?"

Fedvich scoffed and stepped back. He stood straight and held his hands out, "Look at me."

Harry did. Fedvich seemed... thicker. How did he fail to notice those twin swords upon his back? Right, the only sword he wanted from Fedvich was dangling, not sheathed. He swallowed hard. The hope sprang anew as it chased the doubts and fears away. "You joined him. You're fighting by his side. And if you're here... he's not far behind, is he?" When Fedvich grinned, Harry nodded, "You have my utmost attention, Master."

He hadn't been gone for more than two hours. But as soon as he stepped into the hallway where his chambers were, he felt it. Something was wrong. The stench of blood hit his nose.

Harrick ran to his room, nearly sliding and busting his ass in the pool of blood from his two guards, and one of his servants.

"No." Fear took over. She had to be safe. Rylah had to be fine. She had to... He scrambled up, red covering his hands, knees, shins as he slipped and fell a few times before managing to half crawl through the unhinged door.

His other servant's eyes stared vacantly up at him from where they'd broken a table under him, then stabbed him with one of the legs. A guard he knew, but wasn't his had a bolt sticking out of his face next to the shattered furniture.

A whimper erupted from his soul as he stumbled toward his bedchamber. The sheet was dragged off the bed. Blood in wide swaths along the floor and the mattress was a stark contrast against the light colors of creams and blues in his décor. He followed the widest stain into his bathing chamber. Another guard with another bolt sticking out of him lay on top of his crossbow. Then he saw her foot, just behind a partition.

Harry dropped once rounding the barrier, uncertain how to touch, to hold, to plead with Rylah to still be with him. Her breath bubbled, red spilling from her lips with the effort. A moment of relief quickly relinquished to the knowledge she was barely holding on.

"Rick- the baby..."

He looked down at her distended belly, bare to him. His father's brands blackened her taut flesh between the bloody handprints. Blood stained her thighs.

"I do-"

"I can feel... it. Alive. Take it."

He stared into Rylah's dark eyes, their pleading gaze ripping him apart. "Ry I-"

"Take it!"

The command rang out, echoing in the stillness of his chambers, bubbling from her lips. He swallowed, wiping his mouth on the back of his hand and the added swath of blood warmed his chin. He took one of his daggers and walked on his knees around her until he was between her raw thighs. "Oh, Rylah..." Tears dropped on her stomach, washing away the red stains.

"I lo- love you... sweet Ricky..."

He deflated, holding her tight, but carefully, sobbing against her belly. Harrick heard her take her last breath, as he heard the weak heartbeat of the life inside her. He sat up, swiping at the tears, clearing his vision.

Rylah's eyes were already glassy.

He had very little time.

He cut into her belly, careful not to go too deep. Harry adjusted the depth when he saw he hadn't gone deep enough. He sobbed when he saw a hairy head amid the mess of what he made of his most beloved sister. He dropped the knife, his hands slipping over the baby as he tried to pull the child out. When he finally freed it, he cried more.

A girl.

He might as well kill the child now. He watched the baby. So still. Then she moved, writhing before heaving a sharp, gurgling cry. His heart broke.

Rylah wanted to call her something special. Something that would mean hope. A name that would make a difference to her baby's future.

He sniffled, doing his best to wipe the girl clean while still holding on to her for dear life. He swiped down the rounded belly, then paused as he saw the cord.

"I'm supposed to cut this, right, Ry?" he asked the dead woman softly. "Seems like it might make a mess if I don't..." He shook his head at himself. "What is more of a mess?"

He cut the cord as close to the child as he dared, and waited for the baby girl to deflate, or bleed out, or something equally horrible he couldn't think of. It leaked. Thankfully, that was all.

"Let's get you somewhere safe... Lilyanna." Harry held her tight against his chest, the cries gentling with his embrace.

Chapter 18: He's Everywhere! Everywhere! But They Don't Call Him the Streak

For all the gods fucking themselves, how could her luck be this bad? There wasn't a single plan coming to her. Nor was there any way she could outrun him. Where the hell was she in this blasted house?

She turned down the first hall she'd come to. With panic driving her, she bolted through the third door. Where should that be compared to the front? Or the stables? Where were the stables? In the back? To the side? Why hadn't she paid attention?

Because she hadn't planned on running away.

Viscount Harrick Tearney, Sir Redhead, sex god of the whore district, and beautifully submissive even though his eyes sparked in defiance, recognized her.

She pulled open another door. A drawing room? Shabby. She closed it behind her, leaning against the wood. Her legs were on fire, and just when they calmed a bit, too. Helping the Duchess tease suitable suitors proved enjoyable. Relaxing, she thought she found a new friend. An actual female friend.

Until she ruined it all by letting her night life rear its head in the daytime.

No, that wasn't her mistake. That was one tall, muscled redhead with a penchant for pain's fault. The duke's right hand. A fucking viscount who was housed with her brother!

Gods. Let the floor swallow her up now.

Perhaps if she explained herself...

Addy laughed, then clamped a hand over her mouth. The duchess would throw her out on her ass without a second thought. Then the whole of society would learn Adeline Pomm was a whore.

But she wasn't.

She relished control, enjoying being dominant for once. Once every night. The power of seeing men on their knees... of one particular man's desire for her.

I would devote myself to you.

No, not that scene again. Not that memory making her heart go pitter-patter instead of beating normally.

There wasn't an escape from this room. She needed to find a way out. Focus on the moment. Yes, Adeline nodded, mentally preparing for her departure from what might be a haven for a little while longer. No, she needed to get out. Even in a dwelling this large, there were only so many rooms to hide in, and several men to hunt her down.

That was an unpleasant thought. Had she ever felt trapped, like an animal? No. But she did now.

She would never hunt again. It was far from fair to the beast. Her mouth watered at the thought of juicy venison. Well, maybe she'd still hunt a little.

And she needed to help Percy trap more squirrels.

How much had Sir Red told Doxy?

She felt her heart drop as she opened the door. Around the frame she peered, she saw no one. Shutting the drawing room up behind her, she crept down the hall, meeting a crossroads, she scanned one way. She hoped Doxy didn't put two and two together, or that Harry was as honorable as he claimed and kept her identity secret.

No one there. She turned to look the other way and froze. "Garnet."

His chest was heaving as much as hers, that uniform jacket loose over a disheveled white shirt. Her mouth watered at the sight of him even though her heart didn't know whether to flutter or pound. In two strides he was on her, pressing her up against the wall.

But not touching her. She was the one trying to sink into the barrier. Adeline looked up, meeting his gaze.

Fire. Need. Desire. Hope. Everything was in those eyes. He examined her features, as if he was seeing her for the first time.

He was. She wished for her mask as her cheeks heated to the point of discomfort. What was she to do now?

Sam Wicker

The tip of his tongue darted out, and she wished it would taste her. What? She squeezed her eyes shut, forcing herself to turn away.

"Are you going to order me to go?"

Adeline's relief from looking at him didn't last long as she searched his eyes, "What?"

"I don't want to. I want you to order me to kiss you. Or to hold you. Or just to touch you... anywhere."

Her attention turned toward his palms, which flattened on the wall flanking her. He drew near, nearer than anyone not family, nor Fedvich, yet he neither touched her nor confined her. He was merely making her see him, and only him. The pleading in his voice was giving her all the power over the situation.

"Gods fucking," she cursed herself and did what she wanted to do the first moment he crouched naked in front of her. She took his face in her hands and pressed her lips to his. He opened up to her, and she tasted him. She pushed herself against his body, going up on her toes even as her muscles reminded her of the excursion last night. His thick hair slid through her fingers, a metal shard pricked the side of her pinky, and she closed a fist over it. Deeper and more, until she couldn't breathe.

Addy pulled away, dropping to her heels, but keeping her hold on him.

His palms remained clinched, his knuckles devoid of color. She just thought his eyes held desire before. That look could burn forests, and it made her core sweltering.

"Adeline."

He said her name as if he were praying. Worshipping. Much like he claimed her pseudonym each night, calling her a goddess. Mistress. It thrilled her to her bones, much like his kiss. "Say it again."

"Adeline." He readily responded.

"Remember the first time we met?" She waited for his curt nod, "What did you want to do to me?"

His lips parted, a slow smile softening his features, "I wanted to press my face into your chest and let you beat me raw."

Addy giggled, stopping when his eyes widened and gooseflesh appeared on his neck, "And now?"

"I want you to claim me. All of me. Body, heart, soul, mind, all of me. I am yours, so take me."

Adeline stared into his eyes, "But you don't know me."

"I know you well enough. Your voice, your eyes, the shape of you. I know you dig your thumb nail into your palm when you're reminding yourself not to laugh. You bite the inside of your cheek when I defy you, even a little bit. Your eyes widen, and I know I've made you want me. I know your taste now. I know your hands on my face and in my hair. I'll learn everything else. If you allow it. If you want, you can learn all of me."

She was a fool, or this was a special kind of devotion. Love. Yes, love. The moment he grinned and purred 'Mistress Garnet' at her, she had been lost in him. Expecting his nightly saunter into her chamber. Dreaming of what to torture him with all day long, and performing it at night only to do it all over again. He was on her mind constantly, and she didn't realize it until he revealed his need for her.

"I think you have to kiss me again. I need another sample of what I'm to own."

The sound from him before he fit his lips to hers made her tremble.

They were both breathless once the kiss broke. Adeline whimpered when he lowered himself. He looked up at her from his knees. His hands finally touched her, fitting his fingers into hers and cradling.

"Adeline, Garnet, will you please do me the honor of being my wife?"

"Oh no. No!"

Adeline whirled at the cry, even as Harry rose and placed himself between her and the two men. When had they shown up? Fedvich's head tilted, brow raised skeptically.

But it was Doxy, red-faced and shaking a pointed finger in rage, that drew her attention the most.

"No! Bad Harry!"

Jealousy that her brother talked to her Sir Red like that, startled her. She was the only one to speak to him in such a manner.

Chapter 19: Feeding the Dogs

"Bad? I found your sister." Harry drawled, slipping his hand behind him to brush his fingertips over her knuckles. He could not *not* touch her. He needed her like he needed air, and he wasn't about to deny himself a necessity. When her fingers curled around his, it took every ounce of his control not to sling her over his shoulder and run.

"He's not a dog." Adeline's sharp tone made him chuckle.

"He is!" Doxy argued, still pointing. His mouth worked.

Fedvich offered some words: "Get your hands off my sister." The redhead's lips curled to one side, a devilish gleam in his eyes.

"Get your hands off my sister! Why are your hands on my sister?!" Doxy narrowed his eyes on Harry's closeness to Adeline again.

"She's not to be sullied by you, you dog." Fedvich's grin grew sly, his eyes on Harry as he spoke to Doxy.

"She's not to be sullied by you, you dog! Not at all!"

"Fedvich is going to bed me tonight," said Fedvich.

"Fedvich is going to bed me tonight!"

Harry waited on the last one, watching Doxy's brain catch up to his mouth. "There it is," he acknowledged when Doxy's face drowned out the red rage with paleness. "Good for you, proud of you both for recognizing your feelings. Now, don't let it interfere with your duties. If it does, well, we will figure out a wonderful ride and work schedule suitable for you both."

Fedvich's chuckle was dark as he slid an arm around Doxy's shoulders, "Agreed."

Doxy was all confusion and fear. He swallowed, gaze wandering the hall as he muttered, "Dog. Hands. Still a dog. Fucking Fedvich?" He pulled away, turning enough to peer into Fedvich's face with wide eyes, "Funny."

"It isn't. Serious." Fedvich smiled, letting Doxy take that as he wished, like he always did.

"Right, I knew it. Not serious at all." Doxy nodded, returning his attention back to the hound and his sister.

Harry groaned, "Fedvich, you and I need to have a long chat. I'm done letting you just... do... whatever you call that."

"Don't change the subject!" Doxy's finger shot out again. "Unhand my sister!"

"I like her hands. She probably wants to keep them, so why would I take them away from her?" Harry asked, stepping to the side and lifting their joined hands up for Doxy to see. It was a weak tease, but he wasn't about to let go of her. Never.

He met her gaze, looking into those green eyes and losing the present. No matter how amusing a sputtering Doxy was, it was nothing compared to the wonder that was his Mistress. What would her answer be? Why did Doxy and Fedvich have to show up now? Oh, he needed to do something.

"Doxy, as an elder brother of Adeline, may I have your permission to marry her, or should I talk to your parents?"

"No! No, you are not granted permission!" Doxy cried, jerking his dagger out of his boot.

"Well, that escalated quickly." Fedvich said, grabbing Doxy's wrists and pulling them back. He smiled as he pulled Doxy's rear flush with him. "You should make him mad more often. I haven't been able to get my hands on him like this."

"Doxy."

Again, another man's name in her mouth, but this one... it sent a different thrill through him.

"You should calm down. Sir Re- Harry and I will wed." Adeline said with a bite to her words he'd never heard before.

"He's in love with a dominatrix! You can't marry him!" Doxy cried, throwing his weight back and forth to no avail. Fedvich held fast.

Harry watched Adeline flush and was about to try to diffuse the situation when she squared her shoulders and said, "I am that dominatrix."

"Oooooh fuuuck... I didn't see that coming." Fedvich's eyes popped, going between Harry and Adeline. He then chuckled, "Little Pomm, you are certainly full of surprises." He then paused, concern rippling over his face as he peered at Doxy.

Sam Wicker

"Wha..." Doxy managed, his mouth hanging open as the rest of his body grew slack.

Adeline clutched Harry's arm, drew herself up to her full height, and said again, "I am that dominatrix. I am Mistress Garnet."

Silence rose between the group.

Fedvich dropped his hold on Doxy's wrists to wave his hands in front of the Pomm.

Doxy promptly gasped, his eyes rolled up in his head, and his body collapsed.

Harry stared at the boy, then shrugged, "A rather elegant swoon."

"One of the best I've seen," Fedvich added with a nod. He then looked up at Adeline, "Well, Miss Pomm, what are we to do now?"

"Aren't you supposed to be the flirt of the group? This is how you attempt to charm him?" Adeline needed the momentary distraction as the two redheads began discussing how Fedvich could seduce her brother.

Tea sloshed, and Adeline glanced at the duchess to see if she was going to reprimand her brother. Virsin was calm, eyes on Doxy while she sipped her own drink, but said nothing. It was Fedvich who tsked and dabbed the droplets of tea from the intricately designed rug as best he could with a handkerchief.

Harry's arm slid from the back of the couch onto her shoulders, his fingertips resting lightly on her clavicle. Addy swatted his fingers away, only for them to return. She repeated the motion four times before giving up. She glared at Harry, who welcomed her look with a smirk and wink.

"Now then, Doxy, do you want to try to tell me what's going on again?" The duchess asked, setting her tea down in front of her.

"She's-she-she-"

Adeline rolled her eyes, "I'm Mistress Garnet, a dominatrix, and I've had Sir Red in my care several times." She steeled herself for screams and tea being thrown at her.

Instead, a feminine laugh greeted her, and a wide smile. "That's perfect. Harry! I'm so happy for you! You found her!"

"She... oh Addy..." Doxy kept on, staring at his hands in his lap.

"I didn't know she would be so close to us, but yes. We found each other. I want to marry her. I need to marry her. If she... if she wants me."

"No. Not my Addy. Please, not Addy." Doxy whispered, eyes growing wider and wider on his own fingers.

Adeline's heart both broke with her brother's actions and swelled with joy with Harry's words and the duchess' acceptance. She reached for Harry's hand, borrowing his touch to help her ground her thoughts and feelings. Once her parents found out about her activities with this very gentleman, they wouldn't deny their marriage. Would they?

She wanted to marry him?

"Yes, I want him." Addy gasped, her sight filled with a wide grin before she was kissed so hard her breath escaped her again. Men. So dramatic. She fanned herself once Harry returned to his seat at her side. "I uh... um..."

"You will be a viscountess, that doesn't bother you?"

Adeline met the duchess' gaze, "No, not at all. I am a daughter of one now. I know the role well." Well enough. She should've paid more attention to her mother's tutelage in keeping house.

"His lands are..."

"I own no lands." Harry corrected, his fingers tightening over hers slightly.

"That will be remedied, I assure you." Virsin shot back, a sharp look passing from her to Harry.

Fedvich sighed, "If only you hadn't rebelled against your own father, then you'd have all the lands in... oh right, you were The Seventh son. Nevermind."

"A former prince deserves more than the viscount title, he needs holdings. He will. Soon. I'll make sure of it personally." Virsin kicked Fedvich's shin under the table.

Adeline felt like she was grasping at straws in this conversation. Prince? Seventh son? Rebellion? "Oh." She

Sam Wicker

remembered the story. The only reason they'd won the war was because Harrick Tearney turned on his family, killing his own father, earning him a title and becoming a part of The Seven. She'd spent the last few hours running away from him, then molesting him, that she hadn't had time to think about his part in the war.

"Miss Mistress Princess Viscountess?" Fedvich murmured thoughtfully.

"Order of importance, Fedvich. Princess Viscount Mistress." Virsin nodded with a smile.

Harry sighed, "Is there still time for me to claim the fake throne from my brother so she can be Queen Viscount Mistress?"

"That's something we will discuss with our king and our dear Duke, Harry." The duchess picked up her tea again, "And with your marriage, I highly doubt you want to be away at war."

"Right. Can you be happy with being a Viscount's Mistress?"

Adeline rolled her eyes up at the ceiling, "Wife. Otherwise it sounds as if we will not be wed at all."

"Ah, wife has far more power to wield than a mistress, no doubt." Fedvich chuckled.

"Wives rarely use whips, though." Harry said, his lips pushing out in a pout.

"Depends entirely on the wife." Adeline raised a brow, looking to Virsin for assistance.

"Indeed."

Harry's excitable sound made Fedvich gag while Adeline giggled.

"She won't be a mistress. No. That will be good. Right. Yes. Addy... my little Addy..." Doxy whimpered.

Adeline sighed, "Why do I feel like this was the simple part of our courtship?"

Harry squeezed her fingers, "Hardest, dear. I think I can charm your parents."

"Percy is there, too. He's going to be-"

"Not a problem. He likes me." Harry winked at her, then sobered, "But the other two I haven't met."

"Right." Adeline's heart froze, and she listened to more of Doxy's ramblings, "Percy will help with them. I think."

Chapter 20: Lost in Her Embrace

"Death will not come for me this day." Harry reminded himself for the seventh time since leaving the stables at the barracks.

He'd faced countless on the battlefield. Battled angry members of The Seven, including one Regus Norvasos, who was scarier than his father, the former dragon king of Serland. He'd killed his tyrant father and seven of his brothers. Harrick Tearney's heart remained steady throughout all those trials.

On this day, going to his beloved's forested estate and meeting her parents and brothers, his heart was both in his stomach and in his throat. They had a home in the city, but they enjoyed entertaining guests more at their country home. Her brothers were nothing like his. Doxy was nothing like Semir. He wouldn't have to murder a family member, again.

He borrowed a suit from Regus, and the tightness of the pants made him swear his ass cheeks were permanently sealed, while the rest fit him adequately. His boots hid the lack of proper length of the hateful clothing. He should turn back. Change into something better.

What? He didn't know. He'd find something.

The gates were there, and his horse, Festus, trotted through them as if he belonged. Of course, his beast gladly led him to his demise. "Gods aid, I beg." He whispered, making his way down the lane.

A short whistle sounded, and he swung his gaze in that direction. "Adeline?" His breath caught, and his heart settled fully in his throat. He urged his horse over to the edge of the road to dismount in front of her, "What are you doing out here?"

"Your hair looks good down." She said, before her hands dug into it.

"Ah," was the only sound he managed before she pulled him down and claimed his lips. The world faded away, Adeline was the only being other than him. Rosemary and mint filled his nose, and eased his nerves. She broke the kiss, and he chuckled, resting his forehead against hers, "I was going to say, before I was so rudely interrupted, that you look good in pants."

"You think so?" She reached around him, grabbing his horse's reins. Both beast and man followed her deeper into the woods.

"Where are we going?" He asked because if he did what was on his mind, it wouldn't matter if his pants were tight, nor hers.

"Here."

She turned, dropping his horse's reins. She pushed him against the rough bark of a tree. His mouth watered as his hands filled with her when she placed his palms on her hips. "What about your..."

"They're not home yet," Adeline answered quickly, "I told you to come early."

He forgot his worries when her hands made quick work of her shirt. It was off on the ground, and the only thing between her and his eyes was a thin little chemise. The least amount of clothing he'd ever witnessed her in.

"What will you do now, Harrick Tearney?"

His Mistress' voice stirred him, and his grip tightened on her hips. "Ask permission to touch." His mind tumbled and clung to all the things they could do amid the pines and oaks.

"Hm, but you are already touching what I will allow. Now what?" Adeline bit her lower lip, slowly releasing it before she said, "Or do you not like where your Mistress placed your hands?"

"The Mistress honors me." Harry said, flexing his fingers and watching those deep red lips part in a sharp gasp. The mix of innocence and raunch in his love drove him wild.

Adeline's smile was sly, "You may move one hand."

Harry's body stirred more and he hated it, "This isn't a good idea, I'll..."

"I didn't ask whether or not you wanted it. Move one hand."

"Yes, Mistress." Harry cupped her breast, thumb raking across her nipple and feeling it grow semi-hard against his palm. He was touching her. At last. His cock throbbed hard, the pants growing tighter with the little moan she released.

Her hand met his, her fingers working over, making him knead her. This woman would be the death of him. He kept flicking his thumb over her nipple, seeing it grow into the hard peak he desired.

Then she disengaged, pressing a palm to his chest as she said, "Stay."

Harry groaned, fighting against himself with all his might as she took one step away from him. More. Then she sat on a log, legs wide, shoulders back. Her chemise was off, and she was bare to him from the waist up. He took a step toward her, losing himself.

"Tsk." She shook her head, "Take your pants down."

"What?" Harry froze, nothing in his brain but the sight of her chest rising and falling with each breath. The ache for her was both delicious and maddening.

"Show me your penis, Harrick."

"Yes, Mistress." Harry pulled his shirt free, unbuttoned his pants, and pushed them down to his knees. Free from the tight confines, each pulse of blood through his body hardened his cock until it stood at attention under her steady gaze.

"Wet your hand."

He licked, base of his palm to his fingertips, his eyes never leaving hers.

"Show me your seed. I want it spilling between my boots."

Harry took a few half steps forward, as far as the pants would allow. Taking his cock in his hand, he acknowledged her order, "Yes, Mistress."

With a few pumps, she slid her hands over her breasts. Harry groaned, needing his hands to be there instead of hers. A few pumps more, and she moaned for him. Gods, if only he could ravish her. Would she give him permission? When he thought she couldn't torture him more, she dropped her hands to the log, and lifted her hips, rocking them in time with his hand.

His seed spurted, and he felt like a teen watching his first peep show.

Gathering what was left of his wits and his pride, he watched her smile. Gorgeous. If she kept that up, he'd be hard again in no time. She settled back, crossing her legs at her knees and swinging her foot. "Feel better?"

"Yes." He did. The dread from before was nearly gone. The intensity she caused electrified his senses yet soothed his soul and mind.

"Good. Now, tuck it away for me and get yourself dressed."

Harry had to admit, pulling his pants up and re-tucking his shirt in front of a half-naked woman he loved was as difficult as getting a hard cock out quickly. The way she watched him was as much of a turn-on as seeing her bare skin. Love and lust, a dangerous combination for a man to have in the middle of the woods with a woman. Once he was settled, he motioned to her.

Adeline stood, stepping into him, "Now dress me."

Harry swallowed the extra saliva that magically appeared at her demand. He got to touch her again. He stepped around her, bending to pick up her chemise. Pain radiated over his backside, and he grunted, turning to watch her draw back and smack his rear with her bare hand again. Gods, this woman, where had she been all his life?

"Not quick enough." She said as she smacked him again.

He turned, dropping the chemise over her head and helping her arms in the holes. Harrick touched what he could, her flesh was cool against the pads of his fingers. His knuckles brushed down her sides as he smoothed it down. He made a move to grab her shirt.

"Forgetting something, aren't you, Sir Red?"

Harry paused, trailing his gaze over her, taking in every detail, including how the sun caught the gold in her brown hair. "I... what do you mean, Mistress?"

"This needs to be tucked," she said, plucking at the thin fabric.

He was going to meet her family sporting a hard-on from hell. Was that what she was after? "My mistake, Mistress." Harry pressed the cloth to her, sliding it and his fingers underneath her tight waistband at her hips. Slowly, he worked the rest of the fabric in, trying not to pay attention to how her body rocked against his, or the look on her face, or how she warmed under his fingertips.

As soon as the last bit was tucked safely away, he turned on his heel and strode to pick up her shirt. He thought of everything, or tried to, except the woman behind him. Worms crawling through the earth, and the crow shit on the tree, and the seed he spilled at her boots while she... that path of thinking wasn't doing him any justice.

So much failure caused him to increase it by dropping her shirt. He cursed, and when he picked it up again, her hands slid across his hips and backside. Harry moaned before he could stop himself as she cupped the curve of his ass in her hands and squeezed. Her body was tight against his. He wondered where her hand went, until he felt it in his hair, and he wanted to melt right into her.

"Adeline." He wanted to beg her for release from the torture. "Let's run away. Get married tonight. I'll slide into you and never leave." He leaned into the fingertips rubbing small circles against his scalp.

"I like the sound of that, but we cannot." Adeline slid her arms around him, holding him tight against her.

He felt like he could fly in her embrace, or be hard forever while listening to her little gasps and moans. Neither one was meeting her family. Nevertheless, he didn't move until she did, and he allowed her to further his torture by dressing her, the opposite of what he desired.

Chapter 21: Shoulda, Woulda, Coulda: the Regrets of a Dominatrix in Love

Why did she think it was a good idea to have him naked in the woods instead of moaning in her bedroom?

Better yet, why didn't they elope like he mentioned?

Or, why didn't she stay the night with the duchess and see what Harrick Tearney could do to a woman and why everyone wanted him?

Now she was walking down the lane, wet as could be, dissatisfied, and about to convince her parents to let her marry a man of the same station while making sure her brothers didn't kill him. Perfectly glorious plan. She spat and then kicked a pebble among the thousands under her boots.

His new pants were so damn tight she could bounce things off his ass all night.

That would not help get her mind off of fucking Sir Red and into sweet little daughter mode. She could hear his horse's hooves begin far down the lane. He looked good riding. He looked good doing everything.

She ran the rest of the way to her chambers, ignoring the remaining tinges of stretched muscles from the other day.

What would have happened if he'd caught her that night? Elopement? Probably after they wore each other out in the middle of the street and gave herself cobblestone bruises on her ass and the same on his knees.

Muttering to herself, she let Tillie undress her. So much for Harry's dastardly shirt tucking, no wonder he always looked a touch disheveled. Washing off out of the basin of warm water her maid fetched for her, Adeline played through a few scenarios with her family. Worst case, they said no. Best case; they held the wedding this very night.

Was that the best case? The way her mind stayed on him, and the way she warmed when he drew near was indication enough. The sensation of his hands on her flooded her memory. Yes, that was indeed the best outcome.

"That's the dress Mother chose?" Adeline asked Tillie as the maid picked up her underthings and began dressing her. She studied the garment, the fabric thin and a color that reminded her of red wine. Tillie told her it was, and she shrugged.

She had never seen that dress before. Once it was on, she was pretty sure she would never see it again. Harry would take one look at it and drag her to the nearest bed, ripping everything off her along the way.

A square neck, a low back, and a form-fitting chest and abdomen left nothing to the imagination. She felt nearly naked, and that spoke volumes, as her Dom clothes usually had far less skin available for perusal. Tillie styled her hair loose, with a few strands held away from her face with a small cluster of white and wine-colored flowers on each side. She hoped it was enough to hide the fresh patch of scaly red skin just under her shoulder blade.

Adeline reminded herself to take time to get some sun on her diseased flesh before the wedding. She couldn't have Harry disgusted with her once he saw her back and the spots on her legs. Her heart froze at the thought. Perhaps she should tell him before things went too far.

Today, in the woods, would have been a grand time for him to escape meeting her family if he didn't find her attractive anymore.

"Miss, your guest has arrived." Her mother's maid called from behind the door, "I have him in the parlor, and Grath is with him until your family comes back."

"Thank you." She called, giving herself a study in the mirror. Adeline Pomm actually looked like a dominatrix, a shy one, while still in her home. Should she change? No, her mother chose it.

"I'm off, Tillie."

"Good luck, miss."

She smiled a little to herself as she exited her room and walked past two doors to enter the parlor. Harry stood as soon as her foot crossed the threshold as if he had a spring under him. He

Sam Wicker

licked his lips when he slid his gaze down her. Her mother knew what men liked, obviously. "Lord Tearney," she greeted him with a deep curtsy that made Grath clear his throat in warning, nearly covering up the tiny whimper from Harry.

When she rose, Harry bowed, "Miss Pomm." He smirked, straightening up, "Are we truly going with such formality?"

She sat across from him, keeping a narrow table between her and him as if it would make any difference. "As you wish, Harrick." She whipped out his name and bit back a smile when he shifted in his seat. "You are early, my family has yet to return from town."

"I enjoy arriving a bit before I'm expected, gives me a chance to see... more of you."

Oh, touché. "As I enjoy seeing more of you, Harrick. Would you like a tour while we wait?"

Something flashed in his eyes as his brow quirked, "If that is how you wish to pass the time, by all means, show me what you will."

She took his arm, leaning against him and smirking as he grew stiff before they walked out of the room and into the foyer. Walking with him from room to room in her family's home was strange. Instead of recalling fond memories in each, all she could see was how she could string him up or bend him over to punish him. This was not good. Where in gods' names was her family?

They were nearly at her room, the last room of the tour, when she heard the unmistakable clatter of the carriage. Adeline hid the sigh of relief with a smile and a light bounce in her step. She paused as Harry leaned down to whisper in her ear, "Bounce like that one more time and there won't be a meet and greet, but a stealing of that carriage and a bed at the nearest inn."

Grath rushed forward, leaving them alone in the hall. Adeline smirked, sliding her hand down his arm to grasp his hand in hers and drag it down the length of bare chest to the edge of the square neck, "And what if I do this?" Was she torturing him, or herself more?

His breath hitched, "You are a dangerous woman."

"Indeed." She enjoyed this slip in her role. If she'd known how fun it was to touch, she wouldn't have made that one of her unbreakable rules. At least, not with him.

"Adeline? We are back from gathering your brother at the port." Her mother called from the foyer.

"Coming, Mother." She called out, then looked into Harry's eyes, "Ready?"

"No, never." Harry closed his eyes and took in a deep breath, "But for you, I shall weather anything."

Adeline grinned, returning his arm to a natural pose as she guided him back to the foyer. "Look who arrived before you did!" She motioned grandly to Harry with her free hand. "Mother, Father, this is Viscount Harrick Tearney."

Harry gently disengaged himself before bowing low, "It is a pleasure, Lord and Lady Pomm. Your house is nearly as beautiful as your daughter."

"Oh for fu-" Doxy began, only to place a hand over his cheek once his mother's fan left a red imprint on it.

"The pleasure is ours, isn't it, dear?" The viscountess smiled grandly, grabbing her husband's arm and pulling him into a bow.

Lord Pomm stood his ground, merely giving Harry a brief study with a grunt.

"And these are my brothers, the eldest Percy, you know, and Doxy, too. Silac is next, and Mattais behind him."

"Pleasure." Harry nodded and bowed at the last.

"I can't stand this," Doxy muttered, "I need a drink." He yelped when Percy grabbed his collar to haul him back into the family group.

Silac, the tallest and broadest of the Pomms, stepped forward, dropping a rucksack. "Well, whatever he can't stand, I can, except for not hugging you, Addy." He held his arms wide as he kept walking toward her.

Addy grinned, running to him and throwing her arms around his neck, "You smell like saltwater and lilac." Her family was at home. That feeling alone was intoxicating, but also having a new love among them, well, she would be drunk for eternity.

She caught Doxy's glare.

"What are you wearing?!" Doxy cried before adding, "Silac, keep holding her. She's no- ow! Mother!"

The viscountess shook her fan at her obnoxious son, "And what is so wrong with the dress I loaned her?"

Sam Wicker

"Right. Sorry mother. Yes. Yes." Doxy muttered while rubbing both of his cheeks.

Silac chuckled, ignoring the rest of the family. "Well, I have been at sea for the better part of the month, coming back home to you." He dropped her back to her feet and kept her at his side as he nodded at Harry, "I hope you understand that being part of this family means protecting her at all costs?"

"I will always protect her with my very life."

"Gods, no. No. Just no!" Doxy cried, yelping when his mother smacked him on top of the head with her fan.

"Are you two not friends?" Mattais asked, looking between Doxy and Harry while shoving his glasses back up his nose.

They contradicted each other simultaneously, Harry in the affirmative while Doxy denied it.

"He's just shy." Harry added with a sly grin, "Just like... squirrels... are."

Doxy fell three shades of pale, "Yes, friends. He's the best man I know. Honest."

Chapter 22: What Did I Do to Ever Deserve You?

Year of surviving Bertran, Year 1, nearly 24 years ago
One month. That action led to the Vicious accepting him, keeping him. One month of relishing the fact that his father was dead. One month of drinks, women, the king and queen's feasts, Fedvich teaching him new skills, and the lovely decadence that was an orgy with a master.

One fucking month.

"I'm out. I'm done. It's death... she calls me... the sweet sound of her voice has my name in the skies of darkness..."

"If you can still try to wax poetic, you can still run, boy."

Harry hated that voice. Harry hated the man it came from. In the span of one day, he knew Bertran wasn't a friend.

He was an enemy of the worst kind.

Bertran was a trainer. A sadist. And something more than a witchkin, had to be. Just like Regus was a god, or half-god. He already knew Fedvich was the god of sex. And Slayth? Well, elves were elves.

"Wooo! Harry! Run, boy, run!"

He was going to make Fedvich scream his name in other ways. If he survived this torture. He had to survive. He had too much to live for.

"Why do they get to sit and watch while I die?" Harry asked, flinging an arm up over his head to point at Regus, Slayth, and Fedvich sitting on benches cleaning and sharpening their weapons.

"Good question," Bertran's harsh voice turned to a purr. Or what it could've been, if Bertran had not tried to murder them all with noises like those. The stocky witchkin turned his attention from Harry to the trio with a wide grin.

Sam Wicker

"Fuck you, no. Fuck. NO." Fedvich pointed a sword at Bertran, his tanned face turning a shade of green, then pale when Bertran looked at him. "I've been put through my paces."

With a raised brow, Regus merely shook his head. "Rite of passage has been taken by all near. Harrick will finish when you say he is done. Is he done? Is he worthy?"

"I'm done! I have a child to live for!"

Slayth snickered, nudging Regus with a grin. "A child, one."

Regus rolled his eyes, "Not all of us can have a dozen kids, Slayth."

Bertran moaned, "Very well, let's make the new redhead pass out."

"No, no, let's not!" Harry cried, still not moving from where he lay sprawled on the hot stones of the training grounds of their new home. At Bertran's grin, all hope of life after this left him. "Oh gods, take care of Lilyanna..."

Regret. He had plenty of it in his life. On this day, he regretted being born. He regretted his mother being born, his grandparents, their parents, all his ancestors. He'd always regretted his father being born, and the ancestors on that side. That hadn't changed.

He should have passed out earlier. Could one willingly pass out? Didn't ladies do that? Swoon. Could a man swoon?

Every muscle jerked painfully. Even the ones attached to his eyelids and lips made it hard to see and talk with their jerky movements. His fingernails ached from climbing the castle walls at Bertran's command. His hair hurt, just because it was on his body. He was pretty sure his children would be in constant pain if he ever had any.

He was glad Bertran never communicated with his father, otherwise, the witchkin would have taken notes on torture devices and branding.

That was the last thing Harry wanted to go through. He'd escaped that life, and he'd damn everyone before going back to it.

With Fedvich's help, he made it to the second-floor room Regus allowed him to use. He smiled, or tried to, at the wet-nurse as she cooed at the baby in her arms. The little girl giggled, pudgy hands reaching up and stretching toward the woman's face.

Fedvich grunted under his arm as the man pushed him onto the bed. He lay across it, unwilling to move. The softness of the thick mattress hugged him and nearly soothed every ache. "Thank you," Harry said without turning his face from the sheets.

"I'm assuming that was a 'thank you' and not a 'fuck you,' would I be correct?"

Harry groaned, unable to nod. But he felt a shift on the mattress, and the giggles came closer. He turned, staring up at the bright, large eyes of his niece. He smiled, then blew through his lips, making her favorite sound. She squealed and reached for him.

The wet nurse released her, and Lilyanna's little hands landed on Harry's cheek as she wriggled on top of the bed on her belly.

He chuckled, and she opened her mouth wide as if to gasp. Her hands moved all over his cheek, and he realized she was feeling the roughness of his stubble. He grinned, and she patted his face with another wide-eyed awed look.

"For as long as I've known you, I never took you to be one for babies, nor imagined they would take to you."

Harry exhaled sharply, glancing up to the nanny, "Rest yourself, you deserve it."

"Thank you, masters. I shall be back shortly. Shall I bring up a meal for you both?"

"No, thank you. I'll take care of him. You enjoy your break fully, miss." Fedvich winked at the lady, who blushed and rushed out of the room.

He turned his head, working his jaw so his stubble rubbed over her wrist and forearm. She squealed and smacked his face lightly. "Don't bed the wet nurse. She's obviously married to someone nearby. Maybe even Slayth."

"That would be an interesting challenge."

Harry watched his friend sit on the edge of the bed, and place a hand on Lilyanna's back, tenderly rubbing small circles. A thought hit him, "You. You will NOT educate her when she comes of age. No."

Sam Wicker

Fedvich scoffed, "I'll still be in my prime, and it'll be the first generational pair I've taught!"

"No."

Fedvich sighed, "Fine, I won't." His lips twisted though, "Unless she pays well."

"With what money? Mine?"

"You never know what she'll get into when she gets older. Maybe she will want to become a master, too. A Daughter of Gachent."

"She's not from Gachent and no!" Harry cried, sitting up to grab Lilyanna and hold her. He rubbed his cheek against hers, making her giggle again.

"Why in gods balls are you talking about teaching the baby about sex when that's decades down the road? Neither of you will be alive, probably." Slayth stated with a roll of his eyes. He strode in with a large platter full of meat, corn based chips, and vegetables covering it and piled high. Bertran and Regus were right behind him with pitchers of wine and ale in their hands.

Slayth set the tray in the middle of the bed, the men arranging themselves around it. Each one got a pitcher to place in the hole between their thighs and ankles when they settled cross-legged. Harry groaned as even sitting up hurt. Holding the baby hurt. Lilyanna was worth the pain.

He eyed Bertran across the platter from him, "Never again."

"Never say never boy for never always comes true." Bertran stated, pointing a chip loaded with meat, cheese, lettuce, and hot sauce at him before eating it in one bite.

Harry groaned, patting Lilyanna's back gently and wondering how to balance dining with holding her.

"Hand her here, boy." Slayth held out his hands.

Harry passed the infant over to the gray-haired elf, and watched as he ate, played with Lily, and drank easily. "I need to learn how to do that." He frowned, knowing there was little need as he was to pass Lilyanna on to a trusted family. Once they had her for a while, he'd find another one. That way, nobody would find Lilyanna, and the family wouldn't be in danger for long. Or so he hoped. He knew they were about to be sent out again. Pockets of resistance, members of his father's hoard, remained, and they needed to be taken care of before Lily and he could ever find peace.

"Tomorrow, you will meet my wife. She will take the girl for a while until you find other suitable arrangements or until our own is born within the moon."

Harry breathed a sigh of relief. That gave him a bit of time. "Thank you, Slayth."

The elf grunted in answer, crunching a chip loudly as Lilyanna stared at his mouth with wide eyes and clasped hands. Every move the old elf made fascinated the girl. Harry felt a pang of jealousy in his heart, but he pushed it away.

"I should officially welcome you, Harrick." Regus began, licking some sauce and a piece of tomato off his thumb. "Welcome to the Vicious, as Fedvich named us. Please come up with a better name, Second in command."

Harry choked on his food. He hacked till he could shift it to the proper pipe and swallow it correctly. He stared, watery eyed at Regus. "Second?"

The surrounding men nodded.

"Why?"

"You did well during our battles. You're observant, trainable, have a commanding aura about you because of your royal bloodline, and are adaptable." Fedvich said with a grin.

"And no one else wants the position." Slayth added.

"You are his second!" Harry refuted, pointing at Slayth.

"Regus got injured too much this last time due to my negligence. Plus, I'm tired of giving those three orders and them not listening to me. It's someone else's problem now." Slayth grinned at him over Lilyanna's red curls, "Yours."

"Is this another test? Please tell me this is another test. I beg that this be a test and that you are entirely, wholly, joking." Harry swallowed the trepidation before it took over his voice.

"Not a test. Not a joke. You are my second, end of discussion."

Harry felt words begin on his lips, but die half uttered if sounded at all. He looked at Fedvich, who grinned and lifted a shoulder. He sighed, grabbing another mouthful, "Fine. Fine. I'll be second in command. Don't come whining to me when I don't do something correctly or to your standards." He pointed at each one of them in turn.

Regus gave him a devilish grin, "Whine? None of us whines, only you. We get even."

Harry groaned, "Oh, fuck me, what have I gotten into, really?"

Chapter 23: Ever Been Cockblocked by Four Before?

"Silac, dear, tell us about your travels this time while Harrick gets used to us." The Viscountess said as the men sat down after she and her daughter did.

"Right. I started for the Isles of Scales, but you read in my first letter, we were waylaid by this tremendous hurricane. I swear to the gods that storm came from their assholes po-."

"Silac!" The Viscountess commanded with a stern tone.

Silac cringed, "Forgive me, Mother. There's hardly any sailor with delicate words." He then started right back, "It smelled like farts all during it." His grin was toothy, like a half-moon, and aimed only at their mother. "Our new course directed us to the mainland of Kinva. Mattais... their library..." he made a vulgar motion from his lap, "Would be you all day long." He paused in his movements long enough for Grath's son to place the first course in front of him. "And! Father, you would have had to tie Mother down. The men there walked around half-naked, with everything hanging out. It took me a long, long time to get used to that, and that the tits on their women were so perky-"

"Harrick! My dear lord, what is it you do?" Viscountess Pomm jumped in, her pale face flushed and sharp gaze holding her middle child hostage.

"Well, I hardly know now, my tales pale in comparison." Harry chuckled, then lifted a shoulder, "I'm the lowly second to Duke Regus."

"Lowly? My father's balls!" Silac cried, "Are you really?"

Doxy muttered, "I'm his squire."

Their father intoned his balls should stay out of dinner conversations.

Silac clapped a hand to Doxy's back, making the second eldest choke on his latest sip. "Honest?"

Sam Wicker

"He speaks the truth. He might be one of the newest to our Seven, but he has an important role." Harry nodded, his chin motioning to Doxy in the movement. Anything to get the conversation off of himself, or at least the bloody part of his life.

"You're part of The Seven? *The* Seven!?"

Doxy's chest grew three sizes as Silac looked at him with awe.

Percy shook his head, "Here we go. Silac, please, his head is enormous enough. Harry, you shouldn't sell yourself short. You've saved two Pomms, and I might imagine a third... how did you fall in love with Adeline, anyway?"

"You don't understand," Silac talked over Percy, "The Seven are legendary throughout the world! They felled a thousand beasts, saving countless villages from complete annihilation, then they killed the tyrant dragon king, and then they slaughtered these unstoppable bandits who raped women across the land."

"And we can shoot rainbows from our as-eyes," Harry caught himself, still shooting an apologetic look to the Viscountess, "and call songbirds to do our housework, all the while saving princesses from ogres and bears." Harry added with a smirk, "Really, a thousand beasts with just seven men?"

"That's what the stories say. What were the odds then, truly?"

"Twelve beasts to one, and they had another sixteen archers picking off the flyers while their army guarded the village." Mattais gently added, "There was also a fire while they fought, so they did so with limited visibility, breathing smoke, and feeling as if they were in an inferno."

Harry leaned back in his chair, regarding Mattais with narrowed eyes, "King's Academy?"

"I'm a professor there, of Literature and Historical Battles."

"Makes sense." Harry shrugged, going back to polishing off his soup. This had taken a turn he hadn't expected. He still tried to figure out whether or not he liked it this way.

Emboldened, Mattais added, "Harrick Tearney, seventh prince to the dreadful tyrant King Halrick of Serland, became part of the Vicious Seven when he aided our King and Duke Regus, a baron himself at the time, in breaching the major fortresses and finally the palace resulting in our victory. From there, he has made his name and gained title because of his exceptional prowess at Duke Victory's side, thousands felled by his hands alone."

Silence fell, the brothers staring at Harry while the Viscount Pomm shared an expression with his smiling wife. He met Adeline's eyes across the table. She didn't gaze at him any differently than she had before. Relief washed through him as he looked around. He hadn't known he'd needed acceptance until he had it. Lastly, he met Doxy's eyes, and raised his brows.

Doxy sighed, his mouth working as a muscle in his temple ticked, "Look, Harry, I know who you are. How you are. What you do. And I understand that half of it was with... well... and that she... dammit. It's fine. Fine."

"So we can be friends again? I just cannot bear the thought of losing your friendship, Dox." Harry drawled, his lips curling up ever so slightly.

"Don't push it."

Percy chuckled. "Well, that settles it. Welcome to the family, Harry."

"No." The Viscount Pomm steepled his fingers in front of his thick dark mustache, his sharp green eyes flicking from Doxy to Harry to Adeline. "There is some secret here. Have it out."

Doxy paled again, "Oh, no, it's fine. No secret. None."

"That's so convincing, well done." Adeline covered her face with her hands.

Harry cleared his throat, "If I may... there might be secrets every person has that they don't want to share, but I assure you, I love Adeline and none of my secrets shall ever harm or betray her."

"As it should be." Viscount Pomm's voice was gruff, nearly a growl. His glare swung to Adeline, "Daughter?"

Harry turned his gaze on her as well, watched her squirm, and realized they were all done for.

"I'm a dominatrix."

Five bodies leaned forward, toward the same point, but only one asked her to repeat herself was her father.

"I'm a whore." Harry said loudly.

"We know that. They know that." Doxy rolled his eyes before making himself as small as possible in his chair.

The Viscount held his hand up, barring the servants from serving the next course. "Adeline?"

Harry held his breath, and when she looked up at him, he gave her the warmest smile he could muster. No matter what, he was there for her, and he hoped he could portray that without words. He took on twelve monsters at once according to some report or book somewhere. He could take on four men easily. Right?

"Harrick is my client, my favorite one, as a submissive to my dominatrix persona, Mistress Garnet." Adeline kept her eyes locked with Harry's.

It was Harry who watched every facial nuance and movement he could. Fear was not a good expression on his love, and he hoped never to see it again. When Percy leaned back in his chair beside him with a sigh, he allowed himself to relax. Only a little.

"That explains a lot." Percival pursed his lips, "I wondered why you kept sneaking in and out late at night and sometimes at dawn."

"You knew?" Adeline's eyes were wide on her eldest brother.

"Addy, I don't sleep well, you know this." Percy shook his head at her.

"Harrick is your client." The Viscountess's knuckles were white around her twisted napkin. "Is this why you are marrying him, because you and he have already... partaken of one another?"

"You had sex with my sister?" Silac stood, glaring down at Harry.

"Oh, sit." Doxy growled, jerking Silac back down, "He'd kill you with a butter knife as easily as a sword."

"No! I'm intact. I just... well... I um... I know him. Well. Very well. All of him. Every bit."

Doxy groaned, holding his head in his hands as he propped his elbows on the table.

"I would rather not hear such details!" The Viscount said sternly as he stood. "You," he pointed to Adeline, "and you," he pointed to Harry, "my office. Now."

Harry felt his time was nigh at hand. He stood, walking around the table to take Adeline's hand. Conversation erupted in the dining room behind them as soon as the door swung closed. They followed the man of the house up the stairs and through a dark mahogany door. Harry perceived the only means of exiting lay in the entrance or the window. Not knowing what was below the window meant he wouldn't dare risk Adeline as an option.

The Viscount pointed to the five spindly chairs in front of a messy desk full of books, pipes, papers, ledgers, and toys. Harry sat in the one closest to the door.

Adeline whispered harshly, "That one is mine."

He raised his brows at his love. "Is it really that important?"

"I can escape!"

"I have the same thought!" Harry whispered loudly right back at her.

"Sit! Now!"

Harry sat in the chair next to Adeline's. "Yes, Mis-sir." Fuck. Fuck. Fuck.

Harry watched the Viscount roll from the balls of his feet to his heels. He kept his eyes on the small painting in his hands. Then, he set the picture back on the full bookcase, a family portrait with Adeline as a baby. Harry drew in on himself, ready for the onslaught.

"I blame your mother for this."

Chapter 24: No, I Haven't, and Neither Have You

Adeline felt she might weep or scream. She wasn't sure what would occur. A war raged within her. Regret for ever speaking up, and relief in finally letting her secret be known to those she cared for most, tore at her heart in equal measure. She noticed Harry cringe, and straightened in her chair, ready to fight when her father turned around.

How was Mother to blame or involved? Why blame her? Mother knew nothing.

"I assume you found some of her tools once?"

Maybe if she blinked fast enough, she could make sense of that question along with the previous statement.

"That doesn't matter, I suppose." Her father nodded, sitting down at his desk and drawing out an envelope from the third drawer down. "Harrick, her dowry." He held it out.

Adeline stared at the envelope, still pondering if rapid blinking would achieve anything other than make her twitchy. "What?"

She met her father's gaze to watch his brows rise to his hairline and face turn slightly green. "Nothing. I did not say a thing. I wish you a good marriage, I believe you will." He turned back to Harry, "Dowry, son, take it."

As soon as Harry touched the corner, her father shot up out of his seat and was out the door. All before Adeline could resolve anything that occurred in the room since taking her usual chair. Did Harry know what had happened? She turned to him, watching the envelope wave gently above the desk in his fingertips. Obviously not.

She reviewed. Sat down. Father said that, that, and there was her dowry in Harry's hand. Still made little sense.

Harry sat back in his chair, swinging the envelope toward her, "Your dowry, my love."

She took it. "It's supposed to be for you."

"No, it's yours."

She met his gaze, noted as much confusion in them as she knew stirred in hers. One thing at a time. She opened the envelope and took out a sheet of paper. Scanning it, she read what she expected. A gem mine, the new one, untested, and a nice chunk of money via the promissory note. The mine's deed rested within it as well.

"Your mother was a- in the business?" Harry regarded her with a line between his brows.

"I don't want to think about that." Was she? No, not her mother. The proper Viscountess a dominatrix? A nagging feeling held her back from laughter.

"Right, I don't blame you."

Adeline let that stew for a moment as she stared down at the envelope. She smiled, "We obtained his blessing." She watched Harry's countenance change, and it set her heart fluttering. Her breath hitched when he stood and moved in front of her. His hair fell across his shoulders as he leaned down, placing his hands on the sides of her chair.

"I'm going to kiss you, Mistress."

Before she could prepare, his lips were on hers and he took advantage of her gasp. Adeline warmed as he rubbed his tongue along hers, his teeth scraped her bottom lip and she moaned. His hands closed over her hips. Her arms circled his neck, and he lifted her to him, curling her against his body.

"Fortunate I came in here now rather than later."

Doxy's irritated voice made her jerk out of Harry's grasp. "Hm?" She put her finger to her lips. Right. She was in her father's office.

"Do you wish to finish supper, or shall I tell them you're both partaking in marital affairs early?"

"I knew you'd come around quickly." Harry said with a smile in his voice.

"No, I haven't, but I will do what I must." Doxy pushed off the doorframe, his chin jutting, "I swear if you hurt her, Tearney, I will make your pain tenfold more."

"As I hope you would."

Adeline bit her bottom lip before saying, "I need to have a conversation with Harry. We will be back for the next course." When Doxy didn't move, she mimicked his jutting chin.

"Fine. Half an hour, a minute more and I'm taking a sack from him."

"Nghn," he moaned, "well that killed the mood." Harry muttered after Doxy left, leaving the door wide open.

She turned back to him. "This might, too."

Harry shook his head. "Mistress, you could tell me you sport a mouth with teeth down there and I would still want to keep you." He added with a waggle of his brows, "And still put my cock in you, too."

Adeline laughed as she said, "Well, it's not that bad. I don't think." She tapped the envelope in her palm as she turned. She moved her hair to the side, baring her back to him. Watching his reaction over her shoulder, she raised a brow when he acted like he wanted to jump her instead of drawing away. "Do you see it?"

"That you are bare to the top of your ass? Yes, yes, I am all attention, and I'm ready. Desperate."

"No!' Addy began with a huff, "The scales."

Harry's eyes jumped up to hers, "What of them?" His fingertips brushed around the small patch, "Does it hurt? I thought they itched, but only ached when inflamed. If this hurts, then I will make sure not to touch you there."

She couldn't believe him. "You don't think I'm disgusting? Or fear for our children?"

"Far from it. We will worry when we have a baby in our arms who has the disease. Until then..." His swallow was audible, "I may be a mess when or if you become pregnant." Harry slid his hands over her back, down over her shoulder blades, skimming the patch of dry flakey skin, and then circling around her hips to pull her against him. "I belong to you, and I will perform your every desire."

Addy let her heart do its dance it was fond of whenever he said something ridiculously romantic, or he touched her, or he admitted he didn't mind one wit that she had a disease. "We have thirty minutes. What do you mean you will be a mess?"

"Twenty-seven, six, more like." His voice was soft as she slid her hand up into his hair and arched into him. "Less than you deserve for your first time, especially with me."

That was interesting. Did he purposefully ignore her question? "It's fine if I have thirty minutes with another then?"

"Five seconds. Only I belong to you." That purr had turned into a growl, and the hands on her hips flexed, tightening possessively.

"Then why more time with you as opposed to... what?"

"Yourself."

"Oh." Addy pulled his hair, tugging his head down toward her, "Why do all the work when you're here?"

His next noise was a half moan, half curse as he asked, "Why are we not naked right now?"

"Four brothers." She had to remind herself of where she was, too.

"I can best them." Harry reassured her, nuzzling into her cheek.

"With or without your dick out?" Addy also reminded him of Doxy's threat, much as she wished she could take Sir Red to her room and lose herself in him.

His sigh made her body sway with his, his arms tight around her as he rested his chin on top of her head. "While it would be amusing to partake in a naked sword contest, I must wait. I've waited for months for you, so what are a few more hours or days?"

"Months?" Addy curled her hand around the base of his neck while her other tangled their fingers at her waist together. "You found out who I was not three days ago, or two. What day is it?"

"Mistress Garnet, I saw you six months ago and wanted you. After two, I got into your room. Another month and a half of seeing you only every other week, and then finally every week. I suppose you took pity on my desperation and saw me each night, hm?"

"Hardly pity." Adeline pulled his hair, "You were interesting, and not to mention the best-looking man I ever laid eyes on." She thought of something, and added quickly, "Until the hunt, and the tea. Are you sure I cannot have other men?"

"Fedvich is gay, the others are dead."

Addy laughed, pulling at his arms to loosen his vice-like hold. When he let her go, she turned, tucking the envelope into his inside jacket pocket. Sliding her hands into his lapels, she used them as leverage and kissed him. "Sir Red, your possessiveness is showing, and that won't do. But I enjoy this side of Harrick Tearney."

"Harrick Tearney is Sir Red, there wasn't an act once I felt that first lash."

She stared into his eyes, switching from one to the other. With a whimper, she pressed her forehead to his chest. "How difficult would it be to run away?"

"Very," Doxy said from the doorway. "Silac stands in the door now, Mattais is eating all the food, Percy took a stroll to make sure you didn't escape out the window, and our loving parents are currently oblivious to the plans of elopement." He raised a brow, crossing his arms over his chest. "Five minutes to get your asses back in your seats for the next course."

Waiting for Doxy to leave again, Addy asked, "Why a mess when I get pregnant?" A darkness crossed his face, and sadness seeped into his eyes. "Do you not want to talk about it?"

"I should with you. I do not want to ruin the mood, though." His voice dropped with each word, nearly mouthing the last one as if he couldn't breathe with whatever haunted him.

"I'm ready and here when you are, Harrick Tearney. I will listen."

Chapter 25: Planning a Red Wedding, and a Last Whipping

"Why do these ceremony things demand so many layers? You'd think it would be the opposite, as the goal is sex for the night." Harry muttered, watching the tailor closely. The man had too many needles and was far too close for comfort.

He could take a sword to the ribs. Whips to his back. Shards of metal dug into him from his hair, but another man with tiny needles was proving too much.

"Just think of taking all those layers off, one at a time, for your wife. Mistress. What are you going to call one another?" Fedvich said from his slouch on the sofa. He had a scrap of thin net-looking stuff in his hands and was swinging it around, letting it brush his face now and then.

"Whatever she wants."

Fedvich snorted, "Not what you want?"

"No. I'm hers." Harry growled at the pinch to his elbow until the tailor backed away slowly. Satisfied the man wouldn't harm him again, he turned to study Fedvich. "What do you want Doxy to call you?"

Fedvich's grin was a slow growth, his eyes drifting over to the groom, "God."

"I didn't think little Doxy was that devout." Regus added to the conversation when he entered. He paused, surveying his men and the tailor. "I dislike my office being used this way."

"Your wife shoved us in here." Fedvich waved the cloth that was as thin as lace, but definitely was not.

Regus grunted, giving the three men a wide berth before sitting at his desk.

"I bet honey bread that she's waiting for you to take the hint in your chambers, my grand lord Regus." Harry drawled.

"Naked." Fedvich added.

Sam Wicker

"Wet." Harry added, too.

"I just left her wet, but satisfied." Regus shot a look at Harry, then Fedvich. "Don't give him a heart attack. I'm not sure what that compensation would entail."

"Perhaps honey bread?" The tailor squeaked, then hid behind Harry to work on the back of his suit jacket.

Regus bellowed for Fince, telling her to have the cook make the tailor a basket of honey bread for his troubles.

"We have permission to be lewd." Harry raised an eyebrow, considering the mood Regus was in.

"When have I ever stopped you from being lewd in front of others who were not my wife?"

"She has her own lewdness, we can't give her suggestions anymore." Harry sighed, "Not that she ever needed much help."

"The aid you gave was enough to entertain, I'm sure." Fedvich grinned, tossing the white fabric down on top of the variety of bolts scattered on the table.

"How many times was she naked in front of you before you finally caved? Twelve?"

"Twenty, I think." Fedvich corrected.

"Enough!" Regus snapped. He read a page before admitting, "Six, I think, and many, too many, lingerie pieces and dresses that were garments in title only."

"What do you think?" The tailor asked, stepping back.

Harry sighed, moving about in the pinned-on clothes to test out if he could still attack.

"Brother, you are to dance, not run her through with something other than your dick." Fedvich laughed from the couch.

"I have to fight off her suitors."

Regus groaned, "Are you not the only one in society to know she was a dominatrix other than us?"

"And her family? Who might have told others... and they others..." Harry spread his hands wide. "Not to mention that she has four brothers who might change their minds at any moment and kill me instead of giving her up."

"Red wedding it is." Fedvich sat up and studied Harry. "Add another to each shoulder." He held his finger and thumb slightly apart. "And just as much to the cuffs, make them thick and add a pocket this wide to the underside of the right."

"I detest daggers."

"Well, you can't wear your sword to get married in," Fedvich pointed out. "Deal with it." He stood circling. "I think it suits you."

"Do I still have an ass? She liked the tight ones from the other day."

Fedvich grinned, "Oh, you have an ass. On both ends."

He looked up at the sly moon peeking between clouds. "I like nights like thissss. Drinks and more drinks, and more drinks."

"Did he used to add whores to that list somewhere?" Slayth asked, pulling Harry's arm further across his shoulders as the man wobbled between them.

"Yes, he did." Fedvich agreed, then grunted as Harry pulled him off balance for a few steps before he regained composure. "And I don't remember drinking as much myself when he did."

Slayth admitted, "Maybe this will help." The old man smirked, pointing to a familiar place with a single skinny Madame smoking in the doorway.

"Ah, I remember now. We set up something special, didn't we?"

Harry blinked, pulling to a stop and hanging off the two men as he stared. He whined, "She will not be there." His Garnet, he was marrying her. Soon.

"There are a lot of 'shes' in there, how do you know?" Slayth dragged Harry forward with Fedvich's help. He grunted when Harry hung limply from them, his boots trailing behind them.

"Because she's gonna be my wife tomorrow." Harry said with a rather girlish-sounding giggle. "Who was that?" He gained his feet, swinging around to find the man who sounded feminine. "Sounded like a good match for you... like Doxy, nn?" Harry peered in Fedvich's face.

Slayth cursed, pulling on the weight of both men, with Harry's sudden movements yanking Fedvich off his balance yet again. "Why was I to remain sober this night?" He asked the moon.

Fedvich chuckled, "Doxy doesn't have that bad of a silly laugh. His is more... flowy." He made a motion like water flowing in the air, then looked up at the sky with the other two men.

"You drunks coming in or not?!" The madame snapped, flicking the ash off the end before taking a long drag and holding the smoke in before blowing it out her sharp nose.

"Not unless Garnet's there." Harry cried, flipping the old crone off with both hands.

"Garnet? She is here." The woman ignored the vulgarity with a sweet bat of her long lashes.

Harry pushed off the two men, stumbling toward the door and pushing through it when the Madame moved to the side. Leaning against the wall, he stumbled down the hallway and practically fell into her room once he opened her door. He kicked it shut behind him, pulling himself up on hands and knees.

"What if I had a client, Sir Red?"

"I'm your only client. Ever." Harry grinned, sitting back on his heels and trailing his eyes from her boots up to her eyes. "Take the masshk off."

"No. You do not make the demands here." She stomped, cracking the heel against the floor.

Harry moaned, the sound echoing in his head. "Forgive me, Mistress." He loved her like this. In all the frills of black and white, hinting at her pale skin here and there like the slash between her boot and the short frills of her skirt. A week. An entire week since he had seen her last, and she came to him like this. He could barely breathe.

His body throbbed all over when she strode toward him. Her gloved fingers took the loose laces of his shirt and pulled, yanking him into her thighs and abdomen. Her other hand was in his hair, tugging his head back. His heart soared, and his body heated.

"Forgive you? You're in a house of ill repute and to be married tomorrow, Sir Red. What forgiveness is there for you?"

His brow twitched, as did his cock when she pulled hard on his hair. "Could say the same to you, Mistress Garnet." The drink diffused into arousing anticipation.

"Ah, you think you may judge me, punish me?" She asked, wrapping the laces around her hand twice and pulling her other out of his hair. She stepped back once, twice, and jerked the laces up.

His shirt came up around his neck, tightening as she kept pulling. He held his head up, eyes sharp through the disappearing haze of alcohol. "If I have permission, I do." Her laugh made him tremble.

She turned, dragging him as she walked further into the room.

Harry hit his hands, crawling after her, groaning as the frills of her skirt smacked him in the face. So close. All he had to do was grab her, part the folds, and he could taste her.

Garnet sat on the couch, picking up the nine-tails and flicking the thongs over his ass. She spread her legs and pulled him to her, forcing his face into her abdomen. With the whip handle, she pulled the shirt up, baring his back.

The first lashes made him moan and burrow into the folds of her skirts. He slid his hands over the tops of her thighs, fingertips brushing the tight ruched black of her dress on her belly, before she grabbed his wrist. She grunted as she forced his arm and shoulder under her thigh, repeating the same with the other. Harry smiled, sliding his hands up her skirts and flexing his fingers over her lace-covered thighs.

"You take liberties." Garnet stated as she slashed the whip down twice in quick succession.

"You're allowing me, Mistress." Harry jerked forward, groaning into her waist as she whipped him again.

"Giving you a sample of what is coming tomorrow and after." She leaned down, her fingernails scraping up his spine as she spoke.

"Please, more, Mistress."

Chapter 26: Teeth, Tips, and Toes

Percy's idea for one last show was lovely. Seeing his face, hearing his moans after the crack of the tails, and fighting his hands off had been the best night since he found her. Chased her down, more like. If she knew her husband-to-be, it wouldn't be the last time she used the whip on him, but it might be the last she had complete control.

Adeline was going to miss that. Control. Mistress Garnet had command, whereas Adeline Pomm did not. Even with planning her own wedding, her mother had taken the bulk of the choices. Not that Addy had expected anything less to happen.

"Addy, good morning."

Percy's voice pulled her out of her thoughts. She smiled at her brother as he sat across from her at the small metal table facing the garden. "Thank you, Percy."

He chuckled, pouring himself some tea, then topping hers off. "After all the planning, being prodded, and all things wedding, I thought you might need some time. Was your husband sated?"

"Not quite, but he was surprised."

Percy's brows drew together. "How does that work? You claim not to have sex, but yet you are seeing him naked, are you not? He's a big man, Addy."

"There are rules, and Harry is very good at following them. I'm still a virgin." Addy wasn't sure what to think of this conversation with her eldest brother. It both made her skin crawl and amused her at the same time. Was he considering visiting a mistress, then? Just in case, Addy leaned forward to say, "Mistress Emerald, I think you will adore her."

His face flamed as he sputtered into his teacup. He coughed the rest out into a napkin while their mother swept out onto the garden balcony. He wiped his mouth, shooting a look that Addy knew to be 'I'll get you later for that' before giving their mother his most charming, boyish smile.

Viscountess Pomm eyed her children as if they were three years old. "Whatever it is you did, I do not want to know unless someone died, the wedding is called off, or one of your brothers was kidnapped." She waited a beat to see if either of her children would admit to anything she listed. "Good. Now, Addy, we are to begin your preparations."

"Mother, we have hours until the ceremony. There is plenty of time." Addy cringed under her mother's glare. "Or maybe I should go prepare..."

Four hours later, Adeline felt like a goddess. Her skin shone, her body was light, and the dress was immaculate. The goblin she was before her mother's maids attacked was long gone. If only they could have made the patches disappear.

A new one popped up on her side two days ago, and she knew it was stress from the unknown. Marriage. Moving in with the Duke and Duchess until their house was ready in a year. At least she and Harry had an entire wing to themselves.

She smiled, remembering the Duke's suggestion of waiting before marriage and Harry's scream of denial.

He was so dramatic.

"Ready?" her mother asked after fluffing her hair for the millionth time.

"Yes, let's go." Adeline stood, thankful for the lack of a hoop skirt, and followed her mother out of her chambers, into the hall, and out to the carriage.

The house was so quiet; she felt as if she were leaving it to sleep the day away. She turned, taking one last look at her home of twenty-six years. The broken corner on the trellis was where Silac fell when he was sneaking out to see the new twin fillies being born. The single yellow bush amid the pretty green ones never looked healthy, no matter what the expert gardeners tried. A small crack in the foyer window where one wayward arrow had hit from their practice session on the lawn.

It wasn't like she couldn't visit. Adeline grinned, turning and entering the carriage after her mother. The ride was the longest it had ever been between the mansion and the church.

Sam Wicker

Once they stilled in front of the large white building, her father opened the door and helped both of them out. The Viscountess took the arm of her eldest son and entered before the bride.

Adeline looked up at her father when he turned toward her.

"Addy, you may think me indifferent, but I know you have found a good man." He cupped her cheek in his palm. "But if he so much as scolds you, I will kill him."

Addy laughed, leaning into her father. "I'll threaten him with that daily."

"Good girl." He took her hand, placing it in the bend of his elbow. "Another thing; you are to have dinner with us at home once a week, with or without him."

"Father..." she began, squeezing his arm through the black jacket he wore.

"I wanted each night, but your mother claimed it excessive."

Adeline rolled her eyes, giving in to him for now. She could always make excuses later until it became normal for their dinners to be held every other week, or every three. She didn't want her husband getting too close to the rest of her brothers, especially Percy. The eldest held all her little secrets and had the most blackmail. "Shall we?" she asked when her father didn't move forward.

"No."

She tilted her head, looking up at her father's profile. "He's a good man, remember?"

"Still not good enough."

"He's a member of The Seven... and he knows something that could destroy me."

Her father's jaw worked. "I suppose he is the best choice of the grungy lot."

Adeline let her father walk her into the church. When she looked down the aisle, Harry turned. Black and white suited him, and she swore she felt his gaze already undressing her. His mouth dropped, eyes staying on her the entire way up the red carpet. With each step, the world fell away until it was only her family, the priest, and her husband.

The Viscount put her hand in Harry's and left to go sit with his wife. Adeline squeezed his fingers back when he took hold. The nuptials were not of her choice. Her mother wanted the sermon, the priest sharing their love for one another, and more. By the time she could recite her vows, her face was twitching, her feet were aching, and she believed Harry was about to kill someone.

The cheers were loud. There were even fake sobs coming from Harry's comrades including, "I never thought I'd see the day... our boy has grown up so well..."

Adeline giggled and pulled Harry tight against her side when he growled at them. "You're supposed to be positively enchanted with me and the day."

"Yes, Mistress," Harry ground out. "Tell them that and pull out a long whip." He ran his hands through his loose hair and frowned, looking at his hand after freeing it of the long tresses. "I miss my tips."

The wedding party followed them out, around the church's side, to the dining hall. "You took the tips out?"

Harry looked like he was about to cry as he answered, "I was told the tips were a bit much for our first time."

Addy pressed her lips together, wondering how much else was out of her control on her 'special day.' "I'll make up for it."

Her spouse produced a peculiar sound as they proceeded toward their floral seating at the head, moving through the tables near the dance floor. Harry waited until she settled before dropping into his seat beside her. He leaned over, grasping her hand and pulling it to his lips. His eyes sparked with mischief when he asked, "You know that today is yours, yes?" He kissed a knuckle. "It's up to you whether I eat." He kissed another. "We dance." Another. "Or you settle me across your lap and show everyone here what you do to me." The pinky knuckle made him turn her hand slightly in his. "If you want, we can leave." He turned her hand the other way, pressing his lips to her thumb. "Everyone here is yours to command, but mostly me. I will do everything you wish and then some."

If he only knew she planned none of this. She brought their joined hands close, pressing her cheek to the back of his hand. "We have a three-course meal to get through, and a dance, then the cake and drinks." Their guests had settled in during his kisses, and were talking amongst themselves.

Harry peered into her eyes. "I will weather anything for you, but I must warn you... I am a terrible dancer."

Adeline blinked, staring at him, her heart dropping. It was her greatest fear. "I am too." She whispered, "What are we to do! You're supposed to make up for what I lack by being good!"

He chuckled, "I suppose then it will be a red wedding as both of us will have bruised toes by the end of the day."

Chapter 27: Let the Clothing Hit the Floor

Adeline sat back against the soft cushion of the carriage, staring across at Harry once he settled in. The dim light of the single small lantern made his skin appear more golden. She giggled as he wrenched his collar open and loosened the buttons on his jacket. "Are you tired, my lord?"

"No. But I detest people even more because of this day." He smiled at her, "Wife, pray tell me why you wanted all that and not us in bed?"

She grimaced, the carriage jolted forward, "We will be there shortly."

Harry sighed, then held out his hand beside his knee. "Give me your foot."

Adeline raised a brow, but did as she was told. Harry's fingers skimmed over the soft leather of her boot, then undid the laces. He let the boot drop to the floor. Adeline whimpered, and then moaned, nearly arching out of her seat when the pads of his fingers massaged the balls of her foot.

He stopped. "Ooooh... this is a bad idea."

She raised a brow at him, wiggling her toes. "No, it isn't. Continue." After he cleared his throat, he began massaging her again. Adeline closed her eyes, focusing solely on how her throbbing aches were rubbed into submission. When he asked for her other foot, she opened her eyes about to thank him with a smile, but she had to stop.

Harry licked his bottom lip as he undid the laces of her other boot, but that wasn't what had caught her attention. A bulge in his trousers. Adeline raised a brow, "After all this time, I didn't know you had a foot fetish."

"I don't. I have a fetish for you looking like you're about to cum."

Sam Wicker

She snorted, "Well, I haven't looked like that yet." When Harry raised his brows at her, she tilted her head. "Have I?"

Harry rubbed his thumb over the sole of her foot.

Adeline heard her own moan and felt her face heat before whispering, "I see." She stopped his chuckle by sliding her foot from his thigh to his crotch. Pressing lightly, the carriage did all the work for her with its rocking and bumping. His own sounds compelled her to bite her lip to keep from jumping him. "You were saying?" The heat in his eyes made her breath hitch and heart thunder.

The carriage ride to the duchy was long enough that they were both wet by the time the horses stilled. Harry got out, turning quickly to gather her in his arms. Addy could only hold tight. He took the steps two at a time, and his stride didn't lessen upon crossing the threshold. "Get her boots, and leave us alone until summoned, no matter how long it's been." Harry told the butler before striding down the hall. Halfway down, he ran up the stairs to their wing, not even pausing to catch his breath. "Should have ordered the servants to go on vacation with Reg."

"In a hurry, are we?"

Harry groaned, his stride elongating. He hitched her up, making her grapple for a better hold for half a second until she settled in his arms after he opened the door. He closed it, leaning back against it, and finally took a moment to regulate his breathing.

"I can get down," Adeline murmured, patting his chest and trying to unhook her knee from around his arm.

"May I have permission to kiss and undress you?" Harry's gaze pierced her.

Adeline's heart fluttered excitedly. "We're married, you do-"

"I will always do as you desire, nothing less." He smirked, "Perhaps always more."

"You may kiss." Adeline's mouth watered as if she were already tasting him. As he pressed her against the wall, she gasped at how quickly he trapped her, then he let her slide down, fitting her against him. He kissed her, and everything was lost. She arched, pulling, trying to get him closer, inside, something.

"You always make me feel like a foolish boy." He murmured against her lips before deepening the kiss again.

She pulled away, needing to catch her own breath. "How?"

He chuckled, resting his forehead against hers. "Need I remind you of the wet spot in my pants just because you gave me a bit of friction and moans?"

She closed her eyes and laughed a little before replying, "My wet spot is bigger than yours."

"Gods, woman." Harry groaned, sliding down her form until he hit his knees. His hands were on her hips as he pressed his face into her skirts.

Adeline carded her fingers through his hair, so soft, but she missed the prick of the metal tips. She cupped the back of his head. "Shall I show you?" His little whimper was answer enough. There were to be a lot of firsts between them this night. He could actually have her. That thought sent more warmth pooling in her core as she released him to pull up her skirts. "Take them off."

Harry slid his hands under her pale green skirt and white petticoats. His fingernails scraped as he hooked into her bloomers and dragged them down her thighs. He paused, letting her step out of them, before he ran the soft cloth through his fingers, his look devilish. "You are right. It is bigger than mine."

"You may touch with a single finger." Adeline giggled when Harry's devilish countenance dropped to a wide-eyed pleading one. "And you are to stop when I say so."

The way his eyes stayed on hers when he slid his hand up between her thighs made her want to cover his face. Or hers. Then she jerked, pressing back against the wall hard when his index finger parted her lips, and slipped up her hood to press her clit. He kept flipping it, and she couldn't form words. Harry rubbed harder, in tight circles and presses, and all she could do was hold on to her flimsy skirts and do her best to keep standing.

She cried out, her knees threatening to give out with her orgasm. Her body jerked, tightening anew as he kept rubbing. Unforgiving. Then his finger slipped into her, and she shoved her dress down even as her hips bucked forward for more. "Stop."

Adeline shook all over as he slid his hand from her skirts. She watched his tongue lick her juices off his finger. Meeting his gaze, she knew that control would always be handed back and forth between them. And she would love every minute of it.

"Go stand near the bed." She pressed herself against the wall, willing her body to calm down. He did as he was told, turning around to face her again. "Take your jacket off." The heavy fabric hit the floor.

Still struggling to know if her body would hold on its own or if the wall was her new best friend, Adeline dropped her grip on her dress to reach back and undo the gown's skirt. She pushed it down and tested herself in stepping out of it toward him. "Your waistcoat."

Oh, that look, she loved that look. His patience was slipping, and he wanted her. As he took off his waistcoat, it followed his coat to the floor; she did another layer, leaving it behind her. "Your shirt." She ordered, taking her own top off and letting it drop on top of her petticoat. There was still half the room between them, and she had too many layers compared to him. But oh, did she love him shirtless. He appeared carefree, somewhat languid, but his muscles added danger and power to the visage.

Adeline stepped out of her last petticoat and walked up to her husband. "Take my corset off." She watched his eyes darken except for the flickers of flame that seemed to pop up when he lusted. Instead of walking around her, or turning her, he pressed into her body, his arms wrapping loosely about her, and his fingers began undoing the laces.

Bold, the move made her absolutely melt under his intensity.

The cord was in his hand as he stepped back, her bone corset falling between them. He put the tie around his neck, letting it hang off him down his chest. His gaze never wavered from her.

"Your boots."

He retreated from her, one slow step at a time, then sat on the edge of the bed. He tugged each boot off, tossing them toward his other discarded clothes. Harry began to stand, but Adeline held up a hand.

Chemise and stockings were all she had on, perfect to hide her disease, while giving them the freedom to do as they pleased. Closing the distance between them again, she placed her hands on his chest and pushed. He lay back, legs hanging off the bed. She trailed her fingertips up the seams on the outside of his pants. The bulge was back. So, she freed him and pulled his pants off. "Sit back up."

He did as he was told, and she straddled him. Wrapping her arms around his neck, she found it difficult to breathe when his cock pressed between her wet lips. She stilled, staring into his eyes. "Harry, from now on, we are to have as many orgasms as possible through any means necessary, with no permissions needed."

"Yes, Mistress." His voice was a purr as he settled his hands on her hips, and then his mouth on hers.

Chapter 28: Cock Cords for Control and Lace for Losing It

"Adeline?" Harry said, breaking the third kiss since she sat on him. She was dripping, and he wanted to fuck her so hard and fast.

"Hm?"

That little noise was as dangerous as her moans. Harry's cock twitched, and he nearly pulled her to sheath him. He nuzzled into her neck, placing a kiss there, then one on her collarbone. "We might need to tie the string around me."

"What?" she asked as she rocked.

Harry hissed, her heat sliding over him. "Fuck." He gripped her hips and turned with her, laying her on the bed. He made the mistake of looking down.

What were those little flimsy pieces for? Because they hid nothing, protected nothing, and certainly didn't turn him off. He sat back on his heels, taking the cord from his neck and quickly wrapping it around the base of his cock. He had to do something. Anything, because no other thing could calm him down, and all she wanted to do was to drive him past his limit.

Which wouldn't be very far.

He tied a knot that would, should, come loose with a tug on the shorter strand. Harry stilled, sitting there for a moment, eyes closed, and breathing deep. Then he felt lace against his thighs.

He peeked, and he was damned.

She was staring at his cock held hostage, one hand on her breast and the other had fingertips taking the spot he wanted to be. Harry laughed, mocking his past self mentally because the torture she gave him as Garnet was nothing compared to this. He fixed his gaze upon the ceiling, striving for calm while she mewled; his penis jumped like it was going to find itself suddenly inside her.

"Harrick?"

Damn. Damn. Damn.

He gave up, then leaned over her. She arched, and he met her, taking a nice long suck of a cotton-covered nipple. He bit the cloth, dragging it down with his teeth to get her hardened nub properly in his mouth. He risked being too rough if he touched her. He could feel it in his bones.

She was constantly making sounds now. Little whimpers, gasps, half words, and those 'nnns' that drove him mad. Popping her out of his mouth, he trailed kisses down. Her fingers were still rubbing that sweet little clit. He licked them, settling himself between her legs so he could drink her, taste her. He took her hand in his, moving it out of the way and began by getting as much of her juice on his tongue as possible.

His Garnet, his Adeline, his oasis. Harry licked her clit, flicking his tongue quickly, then suckling her. Her hips pressed into his face, and her hand pushed him deeper while clutching his hair. He forced himself to hold on to the bedspread, to not put his hands on her.

He'd never forgive himself if he hurt her during her first time.

Adeline bucked off the bed and nearly smothered him. That wouldn't do either. As she came down from the orgasm, he propped himself up on one elbow, chin in hand, and watched her. He unlocked his other fist from the sheets and trailed lazy fingertips over her knee and up her thigh.

She tilted her hips, turning her leg away from him.

He knew what she was doing, hiding what she thought was abhorrent from him. Harry slid his hand down, cupping the patch of flaky skin, noting how hot it was in his palm. The wedding stressed her out. Or maybe it reacted to pleasure, too. He wasn't sure. Still, he squeezed gently before dipping his head down to kiss a few places on her thigh, and up her hip. Unable to stop, he pushed the chemise up and laid a few kisses along her stomach.

Her hand covered a spot directly under her ribs. He moved it, kissing her palm before kissing what looked to be a new batch of the disease. He then licked under her breast and grinned when her body jerked toward him in response. "Adeline, my beautiful

Sam Wicker

Addy." He swirled his tongue around one nipple, and the other, before trailing further until he captured her lips with his.

The way her legs and arms wrapped around him had him moaning into her. She rocked her hips, and his cock throbbed painfully as her slit cupped him in wet warmth. "I'm not sure how gentle I can be," he said after pulling away from her mouth. He stared into her pretty green eyes, getting lost in them.

"Then don't be."

Harry huffed before chuckling, resting his forehead against hers. "Well, in that case."

He shifted, resting on an elbow and one of her thighs and undid the cord. He settled back, his hips against hers. Letting the blood circulate normally, Harry met the slow undulation of her hips with his, the base of his cock within the folds of her nether lips.

His need for her rose tenfold with a few movements. He reached between them again, guiding the head of his cock to her entrance. He held her hip as he slid in. It took everything in him not to ram into her. "Addy?" He asked, gritting his teeth and staring into her eyes again.

She wrapped her legs up around his waist, and he sank deeper into her. His control snapped. Harry bucked into her, ramming deep and hard, causing her to jerk and gasp with each thrust. Adeline's fingernails dug into his shoulders, and she clawed down his back. Then she fisted her fingers in his hair, holding tight and pulling as if she needed a handle to gain leverage. He was going to explode with each tug. Her other hand dropped to his, still gripping her hip, as if she wanted him to clasp her tighter.

Her cries punctuated each slap of their skin, her heels digging into his thighs, urging him harder and faster.

Harry moaned, hissing prayers to the gods for him to hold out until she had another orgasm. He met her eyes again. She seared him to his soul, and he was gone in the next thrust.

Adeline's hips rocked, as if taking everything he had and wanting more. A few more strokes proved enough to coax out her climax.

He loosened himself from his prop as she pulled him to her. Harry lay on her, panting, forehead resting against her temple. He slid his hand under her, wishing they were one. Her heartbeat was a rapid drum against his palm, matching his.

"Are you well?" He asked after working some saliva into his panting mouth, "Did I hurt you?"

She turned her head, drawing back enough to look into his eyes without crossing her own. "When can we do it again?"

Harry felt himself stir, and he grinned, "Soon, my love." He chuckled, stealing a kiss before adding, "Very, *very* soon."

Chapter 29: Garnets in Sunlight

Sunlight was such a hateful thing early in the morning. Adeline groaned, burrowing into something cozy that shaded her from the light. Her thighs ached. Between her legs ached. Her ass was alight, except for a place that felt like a handprint.

Wait. What was warm in her bed? Her eyes flew open, and it took her a few moments to realize the glistening strands of red hair falling over a golden face were supposed to be there, and she knew him. Her husband.

Husband.

The one with scruff along his jaw, who slept with his elbow tucked under his head instead of a pillow. Harrick's breathing was deep, slow. She was well acquainted with his body. Very well. But she hadn't been able to study him this close, and without him being awake giving some comment that made her want to smack him.

He liked that. Making her smack him, or whip him. And she wondered if he would continue liking that from her, or if he would soon require another mistress. She didn't like that idea. Not one whit.

A faint scar across his left pectoral caught her eye. She'd noted it before, but now that she got a good look at it, she could see it was smooth-edged. Was the surgeon with them that talented?

"Your gaze is heavy."

She jumped, looking back up into his eyes. She smiled as they were half-lidded, those dark orbs with a fire that sparked. "Heavy?"

"Mmhm." He scooted her closer, their hips together, until he pulled her thigh over his. "Woke me right up. What were you so interested in on your husband?" The last word came out with a little possessive growl rumbling in his chest.

"This." She trailed a finger over the scar.

Harry glanced downward, then shrugged. "I don't recall if that one originated from Regus, or if it was from Fedvich."

"Why did they cut you?"

His lips curled slightly at the corners. "They were trying to get me to stop."

She slid her hand up, cupping his cheek and then trailing her fingernails down the scruff of his chin. "Stop you doing what?"

"I'm not sure we want to have this type of conversation this early, Addy. It's dealing with war, and I don't want to ruin your day. I will say that I was enraged. Out of control and turning into my dragon form where it would put innocents in danger." He dipped his head, kissing her fingertips. "I am at your disposal, Mistress. What is it you wish to do?"

He was right; she didn't want to go there. She tapped her fingers along his bottom lip, grinning when he kissed them again. She wrapped her leg tighter, drawing him nearer. "I get to decide?"

Harry's eyes flashed, and he brought his knee up, pressing his thick thigh against her core. "Every day. You get to decide every day what you want to do. I am yours. And your life is yours."

Addy raised a brow. "You know I belong to you, right?"

Harry's chest rumbled, "You are mine, but I will not control you. I am yours, too. All I ask is that I'm the only one you marry, and if you must bring another to your bed, then I'm with you."

She shook her head. "You've lost your mind if you think I can handle another man while I have you."

He chuckled, placing a kiss on her nose. "So, what is it to be, wife?"

"Sex."

"Hmmm, I was hoping you'd say that." Harry dipped his head, kissing her, he dragged her on top of him as he rolled to his back.

In a week, they had left the bedroom twice. It was the eighth day, and Addy scooted up to allow her husband behind her in the bath. She lay against him, closing her eyes when he kissed the crown of her head. Regus had written a line, alerting his second that he and the duchess would not return until the fifteenth of the month, another ten days away.

"Should we have sex in every room and see if they notice?"

Addy giggled as she said, "Harrick, of course they won't notice, but the servants will surely curse us and spit in our food."

"Hm." He toyed with her fingers, resting his hands over hers on the tub's copper rim.

Her body was getting used to the extra exercise. Though she could not keep up with Harrick as he added physical training while she rested. She found she loved watching him go through his sword movements the most, but she adored torturing him during his stretches and meditations.

"Addy, may I ask you for a favor? Two favors, actually."

She tilted her head back, studying his jawline until he looked down at her and met her gaze. "What is it?"

"I need Garnet."

Her heart fluttered. He'd said something similar two days ago, but she thought he was joking. So she'd ordered him about, kept him from touching her, until she couldn't stand it any longer. "I have the dresses in the closet."

"What about the whips and those boots?" Harry dipped his head down, his lips moving against her neck as he spoke.

"Yes, those too." She raised a brow as he seemed to relax and felt the smile against her shoulder. Adeline had some matters to accustom herself to. She got to decide, had all the choices, and Harry praised her for it. And Mistress Garnet was welcome outside of the darkness of night.

"Want me to run from you again?" She asked with a grin.

Harry groaned, dropping his arms to wrap them tightly around her. "No. I couldn't catch you the last time, and now I've added to your stamina. You'll be back at the capital before I could get to the end of the lane."

Adeline laughed, reaching up with both hands to run her fingers through his hair, "When can I help you put the tips back in?"

Harry jumped up, taking her with him out of the water. "Now. Gods, now." He set her on her feet, then stepped out of the bath himself to trot to the closet, trailing water all over the bathing chamber and then their bedroom.

She followed him, drying off as she walked before wrapping the robe around herself. She took the tie, swinging it until she smacked him on his ass with it. "What was the other favor?"

He sobered, turning a small metal box that clinked in his hands as he motioned to the bed.

Adeline sat down. Harry settled between her legs, but didn't hand her the box of tips yet. She leaned forward, meeting his gaze when he tilted his head back. "You're scaring me with this serious face." She watched his chest heave with a long sigh before he began.

"I have a niece, Lilyanna, whom I care for. I keep her hidden to give her the best life I can, to keep her safe from the Tearney name. One day soon, I hope, I'd like to introduce you to her. Perhaps let her reside with us once our home is done?"

Something in his gaze gave her pause in teasing him about already thinking of another woman. She took the metal tin from his hands and slid open the lid. Addy picked a strand of hair, and using the tiny tweezers from the box, fit a shard of metal around the red. "This is easier than I expected." She mused out loud as she added another.

Adeline parted his hair in small sections to make sure she distributed the tips evenly. Sliding her fingers through the thick, long strands was like toying with satin, until the metal shards. When he shifted, she peered down at his hands, noticing him squeeze his fingers tightly together. "How old is she?"

This did not matter, though she desired witnessing Harrick Tearney's nervous demeanor, knowing such occurrences were rare.

"She's twenty-five." Harry paused for a moment. "Maybe twenty-six."

"So, my age." The way Harry stared at her with an odd expression on his face made her pause in adding more tips. "What?"

"I realized only now that I am quite old."

Adeline giggled, tugging his hair. "You can't be much older than forty-five. Right?"

Harry cleared his throat before asking, "How did you know?"

With a kiss to his forehead, she began adding tips to another section of his thick tresses, "Well, considering you are *the* Harrick Tearney, it doesn't take much prodding to get your acolytes to spill details about you."

His brows drew together. "I have fans?" He snorted and shook his head slightly to not bother her work. "I know I'm sexy and part of The Seven, but I didn't think people were actually worshipers of me." He paused for a bit before adding, "Then again, the number of drawers that dropped as soon as I walked into a room should have been a sign, right?"

Adeline laughed. "I want to see that." She sobered a little. "But not for a while. I want you to myself. Unless, of course, you wish to bring Lilyanna now. I must share you with your family. Possibly your friends.

His chuckle warmed her as he shifted to his hands and knees. He sat on his heels, his eyes sweeping up and down her once before he placed his face in her lap. His golden tanned arms wrapped loosely about her thighs and hips. "I need to know she will be safe here, too. I fear going off to battle, leaving you two here and..." His breathing hitched a little, "If anything were to happen to either of you, I'd never breathe again."

"Having your loved ones in one place does not make attacks easier. Who would dare look at this place cross-ways?" Adeline asked as she separated his hair again to begin her work anew in his new position.

He grunted his answer. After she placed a few tips, he asked, "Are you sure you are willing to help me care for her?"

Adeline cupped his face in her hands, making him meet her eyes. "As long as the sun shines, I will always wish to make you happy, and hope to love your family as much as you do."

Chapter 30: Dragon Flight

She stood in the middle of the largest field on Duke Norvasos land, watching her husband strip. As soon as he was through, she placed the golden tag on his chest so it would work the words down his neck, chest, and abdomen. "I'm assuming you're red, like the rest of the Tearneys?"

Harry's grimace spoke volumes, "I detest to be compared to them, but yes, I'm red." As he spoke, he began shifting, walking backward away from her. When he was finished, he peered down at her.

The hot breath from her husband's dragon form washed over her. "You're gorgeous." She smoothed her hands along the smaller scales of his nose, right above his lips. If she calculated his size correctly, he was about the size of her family home. Two levels up and several ballrooms long, her husband was a glowing ruby in the morning sunlight.

She didn't think he would be so small.

She took her own clothes off, folding them neatly and putting them in her pack. Adeline stepped back as her bones and flesh elongated. The patches of skin affected by the family curse burned and felt like she was being torn to shreds in those spots. She gritted her teeth, willing the change to go through quickly. Her scales clacked and scraped, alleviating the pain enough so she could breathe easy again.

Fuck me.

Harry's breathy voice entered her mind and she wanted to laugh, but a growling purr erupted from her scaled lips instead. She shook herself, letting the frills around her ears, jaw and along her back down her tail stretch to their full width before settling in a slightly open position of rest. The sun shining through them made the grass beneath her look greener, and her husband's ruby hue turn a maroon in her shadow.

I should have known you would be green, my love.

Sam Wicker

He rubbed his side against hers as she lowered her head to him, then she bumped his central ridge that started on his forehead with hers. Maybe she should have warned him. No, she should have shifted first. His human face would have given her more expressions.

Do you want to ride on my back, little one?

Only if I can nap, cause I sure as gods don't have a big enough dick to satisfy you during flight.

Adeline laughed with him as he bumped her ridge again. *Let's go.* She took her pack in one paw before lifting off, stretching her leathery wings high and then wide as she took to the sky. She watched Harry follow, amazed that such a large man turned into such a small dragon. He was half her size, literally.

Do you think that our kids will get the disease? She wasn't sure where that thought came from. It wasn't like they were ready to have kids. Were they?

If they do, then we will take care of them as best we can. Harry paused for a long moment. The wind and flaps of their wings filling the silence between them. *I must admit, I fear becoming a father. If I go mad, if I turn out like my own sire, kill me. Have Regus kill me. Someone. I will not put you or our children through that.*

She desperately wanted to hold him. Why hadn't she thought of that? It was a valid fear for him to have. She was sure that the stories and rumors she heard about his father were nothing like the real horror he faced. The pain of the disease she could pass to their kids was nothing compared to the fear he held, she was sure.

While I'm letting emotions control me because you could eat me for lunch, I'm going to add that while you are pregnant, I'm not going to leave your side. Ever. I left Rylah and I... she... I can't do that again.

Lilyanna's mother? What happened?

I left her for an hour or two. That's all it took. I had to cut Lily out of her after she died.

The way his voice broke and hardened at the same time made her heart shatter for him. Men didn't talk like women did, not all the time. It took something deep, heartfelt, to get most of them to open if they would. The Seven and her brothers were the only men she knew who talked about everything and anything. Even her father was verbally closed off until it was time for him to break.

Harry banked east, and then north again, and she followed close behind him, slowing the beats of her wings so she wouldn't overtake him. The forest of Norvasos land gave way to the river, and then an evergreen forest. After a few more hours, that too faded into rocky outcrops of grays and whites with a spackling of hardy plants clinging for life. Then the blackened mountains took over.

Ash mixed with broken obsidian and slate, creating a silt that glistened in the sunlight. Steam rose from crevices. The heat made the air thick and it pushed them up higher into the sky as the mountains grew taller.

Below the ridge parted, circling a valley of rock and stone buildings. Ash filled the basin around the carved homes; charred splinters of wood jutted like broken bones from the scorched rock. Above the mess, a grand castle stood. Turrets broken, a wall in shambles and spilling out onto the city, the once beautiful home of the Tearney's finally mimicked the damaged former owners.

Harry's wings folded, and he dug his claws into a still standing turret on the west wing, tumbling it with a roaring crash.

Adeline followed him, settling stiffly on the round landing pad that barely allowed her bulk to rest within its walls. Tearney's obviously didn't want visiting dragons of other bloodlines when they were in power. That was the longest flight she'd ever taken in her life.

If you want, you can stay in your dragon form. But I thought of something for you. I want you to have it. I'll have to go in. It's not... it's not pretty inside.

I'll come with you.

Harry crawled down what was left of the crushed turret, ruby wings folded against his back. He landed near her, clinging to the side of the landing pad wall as there was no room for him to join her. His tongue flicked out, tickling the frill along her right jaw.

She giggled as she began to shift, the sound echoing back from the ring of mountains along the back of the castle. The clacks her scales made echoed as well, and she covered her ears. Once in human form, she tried to regulate her breathing through the pain. Her skin was on fire.

The ground shook underneath her as Harry climbed into the bowl that was the landing area. Adeline gasped as his tongue raked over her. She wasn't sure if she liked that or if it should never happen ever again.

The pain eased with his saliva soaking into the patches of throbbing flesh.

She stared at him, watching the scales shift and grow smaller as his body did. When he stood naked before her, she wrapped her arms around his neck. He was gorgeous in both forms, but she liked this one best. His loose hair flowed around them in a curtain as he bent down to kiss her lips.

"We still have a ways to go, right?" She asked, trying to stop herself from thinking about what they could do with their nakedness.

"We do. And this is not a place I wish to sully you with, Mistress." Harry's voice was firm even as he kissed her again. "There are bodies rotting in there. Are you sure you want to go with me?"

That killed the thoughts like a rock thrown in a pond. "Yes?"

Harry lifted her pack. "Get dressed. And pull out a handkerchief and douse it in perfume or something."

She did as she was told, except she didn't have perfume with her. Adeline followed Harry through the tall doors hanging off their hinges comically. He carried both of their bags on his back, and moved with a grace she couldn't have managed under the weight. When he stepped over the first rotten body, Adeline nearly gagged, for that's the exact moment she took in a deep breath through her nose instead of her mouth.

She bumped into her bag when he came to a stop.

"Last chance to turn back, my wife."

Adeline straightened her spine. "I won't leave you alone in this place." His wicked grin sent a chill down her spine.

"It's better being alone or with you in this place than the alternative."

Chapter 31: Inheritance

Adeline breathed in deep once she was out on the balcony of the emptiest room they'd crossed in the castle. The air had never smelled so sweet. She turned when she heard Harry move around in the room behind her. She watched him step over a swath of brown. It had probably once been red. Bile rose for the millionth time, and for the same number of times she swallowed it down.

How could he be so collected? Was this normal to him? If this was better than what was here before... no. She couldn't think of that. She wouldn't until he was ready to talk about it because her speculations didn't help either of them.

When her husband appeared again, he had moved both bags to one shoulder and a plain wooden box was tucked under his other arm. He dropped the bags at the door, and strode toward her. His brows drew together over his dark eyes with each step until he cupped her cheek in one hand. "It's alright if you need to throw up."

She shook her head, then leaned into his touch.

"Stubborn."

"You married me."

Harry chuckled, "And I'd do it again if you were twice as stubborn as you are now." He put the box on the balustrade beside them and cupped her face with both hands as he kissed her again. "Thank you."

"For what?" Adeline asked, watching something flicker in his gaze.

"Being with me, here, not letting me drift alone in darkness."

Adeline wrapped her arms around his neck and drew him into a hug. "I don't want to ever be anywhere else."

Sam Wicker

Harry drew back, kissing her forehead. He grabbed the box with one hand, right over a stain in red. His handprint in blood. He opened it so she could see inside with him.

Within was a jumble of rings and necklaces beside two thin packets on top of one another. Jewels of reds and blues were set in the loose jewelry. It was the packets he pulled out before setting the box to the side again.

"This one is for Lilyanna. It was Rylah's favorite." Harry stated as he untied the ribbon and unwrapped a silver chain with a thumb sized blue sapphire hanging from it.

"It's so pretty. No wonder she loved it." Adeline folded her hands in front of her so she wouldn't touch the stone. She watched intently as Harry placed it back, and retied the ribbon gently around the silk cloth.

"This is for you." Harry stated, untying the next one. He pulled out another silver chain. Hanging from it was a cluster of red and purple gemstones set within a melted mess of silver, gold, and copper. It was wild, untamed, and each time it turned it revealed something new.

Adeline didn't have words. Her eyes burned with unshed tears, "Are you sure? Don't you want to keep it for yourself?"

He snorted before putting Lilyanna's in his pocket and tossing the empty cloth over his shoulder. He placed the necklace over her head, settling it around her neck after pulling her hair out from under the chain. "This was my mother's." He pressed his thumb against a purple stone, "Her." He then moved it over to a red one, "And I." He then turned the necklace, pointing to a tiny green stone nestled between two larger red ones, "And you."

Adeline giggled, "Your favorite people, especially yourself since there's more red than anything."

Harry laughed as he said, "You know me so well, my love."

"She's going to hate me." Adeline knew it. She felt it in her bones. She tied her hair up, then pulled it back down. She went through her pack to pull out a dress, then thought better of it and shoved it back in. Her pants were good for running away should Lilyanna detest her.

She froze when Harry's hands rested on her hips. She straightened, leaning against him as he wrapped his arms about her. "I know."

"You know you're being ridiculous?"

His lips tickled her earlobe and she jerked away from them. "It's not ridiculous!"

"It is, because she already loves you."

Adeline turned to study him. "How so?"

"Because she said so in her last letter." Harry said with a smirk.

"Because you wrote about me. When?"

"When you were asleep mostly."

Adeline groaned, "So what? She knows every mark on me and how many times you've made me scream your name?"

Harry's face twisted as he shook his head, "If she loved you because of that we would have an issue to discuss with her." He patted her backside, then squeezed her ass. "She loves you because I love you. That's enough for her." He stopped rubbing her, "Oh, and we're wandering… somethings. Wanderers."

"What?" Adeline raised a brow at him. "Wanderers? Why?"

"She doesn't need to know that I kill for a living. Well, she will eventually, but for now, we wander about doing things."

Adeline pressed her lips together and pulled them between her teeth as she regarded her husband. He was picking up their packs, and then raking a hand through his loose hair to get it free of the straps. How foolish did he believe this girl to be? "And what are The Seven?"

Harry grinned, "You don't want to know and she won't ask. She's heard the stories too many times."

"What stories?"

Harry tapped a finger on his chin. "The stories about The Seven making the world beautiful in their own way."

"Gods, you fed her nursery stories of your great battles?" Adeline hugged herself, trying to think of anything else so she wouldn't make a fool of herself laughing until she peed her pants.

He deflated, kicking a dried leaf in the grass. "She was little and I told her stories. Then she wanted to hear them over and over again. I didn't have the heart to tell her that I'm not a wandering

Sam Wicker

storyteller who brightens kids' days by rhyming with whip snaps to keep time."

Adeline covered her face in her hands, "You made The Seven a circus act?"

"Well, when you put it that way... yes? We do have a few dance numbers learned."

She crouched, giving in as images of Regus in an overly furred costume wrestling a bear, Fedvich's acrobatics to ridiculous music, and Charn's pitched singing goading Harry's own stories flooded her mind. She couldn't imagine Bertran or Slayth doing anything of the sort. Doxy. What would her brother be? The laughingstock the rest of the men chased in and out of the arena? She couldn't breathe she was trying so hard to hold it in.

"Mistress?"

She whimpered, planting her face on her knees and hugging her legs to her as she balanced in her crouched position.

"Why did you break her before she could meet me, Uncle Harry? And why did you call her Mistress?"

"Lily! You're getting better at sneaking up on people!" Harry cried.

Adeline heard the rustling of boots in grass and Lilyanna's light giggles. She looked up, watching the two, and her heart warmed. This was her family. Her choice.

Chapter 1: What Is Life? Baby Don't Hurt Me...

All he needed to do was cross the threshold. Safety lies beyond that very door. He just needed to get up the steps. Why were there so many steps? Why did the path take forever between the training grounds and the duke's front door?

No matter. One fucking step at a time. One more step. Another.

What was life? Another step.

There had to be another war somewhere. That was better than this hellish scape. Wasn't it?

No.

One more step. Nope, we're not falling backwards. Always move forward. Never leave your comrades open. There it was, forward a step. Good boy.

Five more fucking steps. Weren't there five to begin with? Had he moved?

He turned, looking back down and counting. Five. He looked up. Five. What the fuck?

He groaned, reaching down to lift one twanging thigh up to the next step, then the other. "Come on boys, don't let me down now." Since when were his thighs boys?

Probably since everyone had a dick in a cunt and didn't want to leave it. That was sound logic. Hope sprang eternal as he crested the last step. Flat, it was flat from here on out, he could do it. Everything was within reach.

He stumbled forward as the muscles in his legs screamed in protest. He was wet all over, absolutely sticky, and he could smell himself. Literally smell himself and he did not smell. Not Fedvich. Things *on* him smelled like the blood of his enemies, cum, the shit on the streets if he didn't sidestep it in time.

Fedvich DeLorraine Gavaintch made it inside. Heaven was nigh. He looked toward the right where he knew the second was housed and cursed as his eyes trailed up the stairs. "Fuck this." He allowed himself to melt to the polished stone floor. "Harry!" He bellowed because his voice was the only thing that properly worked. "Get your dick out of your wife and down here!"

The stone floor felt lovely against his sweaty skin. He could die happy here. Cooled down, not running, not listening to two hundred other men panting and not getting any pleasure from it. Yes, heaven was indeed nigh if it existed.

Where were the servants? Oh yeah, that was right. When the actual mister and mistress of the house was away the mice played. "Harrick! Tearney!" He bellowed again.

"What do you want... Fedvich?"

He was running down the stairs, Fedvich could hear him. He missed being able to move freely, without the constraint of sore muscles and sorer pride. How was it that the whore and the vicious got partners before he did?

The sun got to him; that was the only explanation of why his mind was wandering, skipping all over the place like a child with a basket of flowers and not a care in the world.

"What are you doing?"

At least Harry had the decency to crouch down in front of his face. What he didn't have the decency of doing was getting dressed properly. Fedvich stared at the thighs, then cock and balls displayed in a towel just for him to see.

"Hating you." The man had the audacity to chuckle and slap him on the back. That was sore there, too. He sighed, "While you have a perfectly nice set, they are not for me, therefore I don't wish to stare at your dick and sack. Move!"

Harry grumbled but did as he was told, sitting on the floor in front of his comrade, adjusting the towel so he wasn't flashing anyone.

"Come back. Please come back."

"You just told me you didn't want to see my dick and balls and now you do?"

"I don't want those to come back! I want you or Regus to get your asses back to us! You know? The men, me, the soldiers who need training and my sanity that needs kept and I really don't want to die this young because I have so much to do."

"Like what?"

Fedvich should have felt insulted, but he didn't because Harry obviously has less to do with his life than he did. "Figure out what it is about cunts that have you and Regus stay in them. Or find a partner who is more than a one night stand or... relief through dry spells."

Harry lay down, his feet pointing in the opposite direction from Fedvich's so they faced one another upside down. "What is wrong?"

"This is weird. Why are you lying there when I don't like you that much?" Fedvich stared at Harry's features. In the two weeks that he'd not seen Harry, his face hadn't changed much. But there was still a little something he couldn't quite put his finger on. "What's wrong is Bertran is in charge."

"He's been in charge before-"

"Not for this long!" Fedvich's blood boiled, "Do you know how many miles we ran today? Do you? Do you know how many drill sets we had to do *while* running those miles because Bertran has this rule that no one can fall more than three paces behind everyone? Huh?"

"It can't be that bad."

Fedvich wanted to spit in that smug face, "You run to the capital and back and do six sets of fifty."

"To the capital?!"

Fedvich and Harry both lifted their heads enough to study the woman in a robe standing at the end of the staircase.

"Hello little Pomm." Fedvich smiled, resting his chin on the floor, then glared at her because she was the reason for his current state. In a way. "Stop seducing Harry. Or fucking him. Whatever it is you're doing, stop it. At least until Regus gets back."

Adeline smiled sweetly, "That's not happening anytime soon, Fedvich." As she crooned those terrible words in her sweet voice, she made her way to him.

He was about to beg, truly beg, when she sat on his ass. Concern; that was a new feeling when a woman sat on him. His eyes slid toward Harry. Fear; that wasn't new when a woman sat on him and her man was nearby. "Oh... oh gods..." he moaned, melted, and wanted to have her babies all at once. The woman's hands were magic, smoothing the pain away from his lower back and working up.

He whimpered, then words began pouring out of his mouth and he didn't care what he said or didn't say. "Adeline, I worship you with my whole entire black heart. You don't deserve an ass like Harry's, you need a better one, I'll find you one. Swear it. You can have mine. Me. All of me with those hands, my dearest little Pomm. I will fucking give you everything I own. The clothes off my back, my hair, everything, just so long as you don't stop."

"She's a Tearney."

"She's better than a Tearney!"

"Boys, I'm a Pomm Tearney, you're both right."

Fedvich heard himself make the oddest sound as pain shot through his back and down his arm when she pushed a particular spot on his shoulder, "Oh Pomm, please don't hurt me like that anymore." He groaned when she stopped, "But don't stop."

"Is there a reason why all members of the seven love pain?" Addy asked, returning to her administrations.

"Have you met Regus?" Both men asked at the same time.

Acknowledgements

I want to thank everyone who reads this, first and foremost. Without you, I wouldn't have the desire to keep writing. Thank you, and I hope you stay with these characters of mine whether you love them, hate them, or want to lick them.

Next, to my husband: you are the best. You know what you do... from the long conversations of me talking about these characters to you having to fix something I broke on the computer to just holding me while I doubt myself... I couldn't do this without you. I couldn't Life without you.

To my beta readers, fellow authors, and the Authortube community on YouTube: here we go again. Thank you! You're so supportive and awesome. I'm glad we found one another.

About the Author

Sam Wicker is a small-towner, married to a loving and the most supportive husband ever, and they have a furbaby named Kona. She's always wanted to write stories full of romance, real people doing fantastical things, and animals that awe. Sam hopes her stories inspire those suffering from anxiety and gives all her readers a place to escape to.

Her books are: Romantasy, Fantasy Romance, Romantic Comedy Fantasy, Dark Romantic Comedy Fantasy, Urban Fantasy Adult - sexual content on page

www.ingramcontent.com/pod-product-compliance
Lightning Source LLC
Chambersburg PA
CBHW060455300726
48975CB00008B/2525